"I'm here to interview for the nanny position," Bailey ventured nervously.

Gib Harden had on a plain white T-shirt that didn't look plain at all, hugging his broad shoulders and well-muscled chest. He also wore jeans tight enough to cling to his narrow waist, even with a leather tool belt strapped around his lean hips.

But the tool belt, Bailey suddenly noticed, didn't have tools in it. Instead, poking out of its pockets were a rag doll, a clean disposable diaper, talcum powder, wet wipes, a toddler's juice cup and a baby bottle.

Bailey fought a laugh at the incongruous sight. Then felt a funny jolt in the vicinity of her heart.

For this sexy single dad was big. Tall. Powerfully built. All in all, there was nothing about him that didn't shout rugged, pure, potent masculinity.

Except the contents of his most intriguing tool belt…

Dear Reader,

Fall is in full swing and so is Special Edition, with a very special lineup!

We begin this month with our THAT'S MY BABY! title for October. It's a lesson in instant motherhood for our heroine in *Mom for Hire*, the latest story from the popular Victoria Pade.

Three veteran authors will charm you with their miniseries this month. CUPID'S LITTLE HELPERS is the new series from Tracy Sinclair—don't miss book one, *Thank Heaven for Little Girls*. For fans of Elizabeth August, October is an extraspecial month— *The Husband* is the latest emotional and compelling title in her popular SMYTHESHIRE, MASSACHUSETTS series. This series began in Silhouette Romance and now it is coming to Special Edition for the very first time! And Pat Warren's REUNION series continues this month with *Keeping Kate*.

Helping to round out the month is *Not Before Marriage!* by Sandra Steffen—a compelling novel about waiting for Mr. Right. Finally, October is premiere month, where Special Edition brings you a new author. Debut author Julia Mozingo is one of our Women To Watch, and her title is *In a Family Way*.

I hope you enjoy this book, and all of the stories to come!

Sincerely,

Tara Gavin,
Senior Editor

Please address questions and book requests to:
Silhouette Reader Service
U.S.: 3010 Walden Ave., P.O. Box 1325, Buffalo, NY 14269
Canadian: P.O. Box 609, Fort Erie, Ont. L2A 5X3

VICTORIA PADE
MOM FOR HIRE

Silhouette ®

SPECIAL ▼ EDITION ®

Published by Silhouette Books
America's Publisher of Contemporary Romance

SILHOUETTE BOOKS

ISBN 0-373-24057-0

MOM FOR HIRE

Books by Victoria Pade

Silhouette Special Edition

Breaking Every Rule #402
Divine Decadence #473
Shades and Shadows #502
Shelter from the Storm #527
Twice Shy #558
Something Special #600
Out on a Limb #629
The Right Time #689
Over Easy #710
Amazing Gracie #752
Hello Again #778
Unmarried with Children #852
Cowboy's Kin #923
Baby My Baby #946
Cowboy's Kiss #970
Mom for Hire #1057

*A Ranching Family

VICTORIA PADE

is a bestselling author of both historical and contemporary romance fiction, and mother of two energetic daughters, Cori and Erin. Although she enjoys her chosen career as a novelist, she occasionally laments that she has never traveled farther from her Colorado home than Disneyland, instead spending all her spare time plugging away at her computer. She takes breaks from writing by indulging in her favorite hobby—eating chocolate.

To Become the Perfect Mother You Should...

1) Be determined. You need instant experience. No sweat—just find a frazzled young father who needs a nanny, *fast!*

2) Be creative. Make up a likely story why you had to order dinner from the local pizza parlor—*again.* Never admit you couldn't cook a meal to save your life.

3) Be patient. Especially when one of the kids builds a sandbox on the dining room table and another is hiding a frog in the toilet tank.

4) Be focused. Your only goal is to gain experience. Becoming attached to the children or their gorgeous "dad" could be fatal!

5) Be strong. Whatever you do, *don't* fall in love!

Chapter One

"I want to have a baby," Bailey Coltrain announced.

She and Jean Oslin were standing in front of the sinks and mirrors in the restroom of a restaurant near the University of Colorado's medical center. They'd just taken turns at the podium for lectures to a medical conference on managing heart conditions in pregnant women. They were on their lunch break.

"You want to *have* a baby?" Jean asked incredulously.

Bailey didn't take offense at the tone. Jean was her best friend. They owned the office building that housed Bailey's gynecology and obstetrics practice on one side and Jean's cardiology practice on the other.

"Right. I want to have a baby of my own." Bailey ran a comb through her just-below-the-chin-length walnut-colored hair, even though every strand of the bob was already in place.

"You want to *have* a baby of your own?" Jean parroted yet again, more incredulously than the time before, staring at Bailey in the mirror. Her dark eyes were wide as she ignored her own short, prematurely salt-and-pepper hair, even though it could have benefited from a combing more than Bailey's.

"That's what I said, Jean. Is the buzz of that sound system still ringing in your ears or what?"

"I'm hearing you. I just can't believe what I'm hearing."

"I know," Bailey said, anticipating what her friend was getting at. "I'm not married—"

"Or even involved with anyone."

"Or looking at an intimate relationship on the horizon. That's the point. I'm thirty-five years old. I deliver other people's babies day in and day out. I want one of my own. I'm thinking of being artificially inseminated."

"Oh my God."

"I'm just saying that I'm established in my career. Making good money. Healthy. Happy. And ready. I can't help it if Mr. Right-and-Wonderful hasn't come down the pike. And I can't keep waiting for him to." She applied a little light pink gloss to her lips.

Jean was still staring somewhat slack-jawed.

"What?" Bailey demanded impatiently.

"You're a good physician, Bailey. One of the best around. But let's face it—if Marguerite quit working for you tomorrow, you couldn't make yourself a cup of tea, let alone take care of a child. You kill goldfish—"

"Only a few. I was just too busy to remember to feed them. I had the tank taken out of my office and put in the waiting room for the receptionist to take care of."

"My point exactly."

"I wouldn't forget to feed them if they were children, Jean."

"No? I'm not so sure about that. Sometimes you forget to feed yourself. And what about things like cleaning up after a kid? Cleaning is not your forte, either. In fact, you told me yourself that you've never done it. In your *entire life*. Never dusted a table. Never cooked a meal. Never washed a load of laundry. Never—"

"Okay, so I'm not domestic."

"In the extreme."

"It isn't my fault I grew up the way I did."

"I know. Mom a neurologist. Dad a cardiac surgeon. Hanging around hospitals with them while they paid people to keep the home fires burning. Just the way you pay Marguerite to do. But, Bailey—"

"So maybe having a baby will domesticate me."

"Poor baby. Poor, poor baby."

"I beg your pardon."

"You never baby-sat as a kid. Have you ever so much as changed a diaper?"

"No, but—"

"You didn't have any brothers or sisters. You said yourself you didn't do well on your pediatric rotation as an intern because you didn't know how to relate to children. That you really didn't even have friends your own age growing up, that you followed the hospital janitor for fun. And now you think you can have and raise a kid of your own?"

"Okay, so I had an unusual childhood. That's part of why I'm feeling the itch for a baby myself now—to have a taste of everything I missed. To give my own kid the kind of childhood I wish I'd had."

"You know what I think?"

"I know you'll tell me."

"I think you're having some kind of early midlife crisis. First you stop taking maternity patients nine months ago so you wouldn't have any deliveries and could take off for the next three months. To *Africa,* of all places. And now you want to get pregnant. These things are a little extreme, Bailey."

"Okay, so I've been feeling restless and discontented the past year since losing my folks. You said it yourself—I've been enmeshed in medicine in one way or another my whole life. I don't *have* any other life, especially not now that Mom and Dad are gone. You have Harvey. You have kids. You have more than your work. That's what I want, too. I've had lousy luck with men, but I can have a baby without one. And I want to. I'm *going* to."

Jean's eyebrows arched. "So this is a definite decision? You aren't just thinking out loud?"

"No, I'm not just thinking out loud." In fact, this was something she'd been thinking about for a long while. Something she'd been craving for a long while. And yes, she realized at that moment, she had made up her mind. She was going to do it.

She watched her friend's expression soften. "It isn't that I don't understand, Bailey. I've said it to Harvey a million times—I wouldn't have wanted to grow up the way you did or go home to nobody but a housekeeper every night now. But a baby, Bailey. A *baby.*

You just don't know what an undertaking that is. Especially on your own, a single parent.''

"I've thought about that, and I'm okay with it."

"You can't be okay with something before you have any idea what it entails."

Bailey rolled her eyes at her friend.

"I'm serious. Don't think domestication comes like a bolt of lightning when you're in the stirrups on the delivery table. It doesn't. If you want to be a mommy, you'd better know you can wash those cute little rompers it'll spit up on. You'd better know you can cook up a whole variety of things it can smear in its hair. You'd better know you can swab out the toilet it pours varnish into. And you'd better know it *before* you have it. Otherwise you'll be doing a major disservice to that child by bringing it into the world hoping you can always hire someone else to do the dirty work because you don't have the foggiest idea how to do it yourself."

Jean disappeared into one of the bathroom's stalls and Bailey powdered her straight, somewhat thin nose. Then she ran the tip of her ring finger under one pale blue eye as if that might erase the tiny, almost invisible line that wasn't a wrinkle yet but would be ten years from now. She had spent her thirty-fifth birthday *alone* this year, and recently she'd been thinking more and more about that. And about living her whole life without a family of her own. Isolated in the same kind of sterile world she'd grown up in. Except even then, she'd had her parents.

Bailey turned to face the full-length mirror on the side wall to see if her new navy blue pantsuit was holding up under the hours of sitting, listening to speeches.

When this conference was over today, Jean would head home to her husband and her two teenagers. Bailey would go home to a house left clean by Marguerite, her housekeeper. Clean and empty. And much, much too quiet.

She cast a glance at the door to the stall Jean had gone into. Since it was still closed and she had a bit of privacy, she turned in profile to the full-length mirror. She pulled her jacket tight across her flat stomach, arched her back to try for a semblance of a pregnant tummy, laid her hand there the way she'd seen so many of her expectant mothers do and tried to imagine what it would feel like to have a child growing inside her own womb.

She thought that if she did, she could go home tonight all alone and happily spend the whole evening just feeling it move inside her. Feeling that special connection to someone. To her own flesh and blood.

How hard could domesticity and parenthood be? If she could deliver a baby she could certainly care for one.

But maybe Jean was right. Maybe she should get in some practice beforehand. She owed her future child that. So she'd be prepared when it got here. So she'd be the best mother she could be, with hired help or without it.

Bailey heard the toilet flush and gave her abdomen one last press—wishing hard that there was a baby growing there already. Then, just as Jean came out, she straightened up and smoothed the wrinkles out of her suit as if that's all she'd been doing in the first place.

"So where do you suggest I go to get domesticated *before* I have a baby?" she asked her friend as Jean washed her hands.

"How do I know? Maybe you can borrow one of Marguerite's grandkids and get her to give you lessons. Nothing like firsthand experience to learn the ropes."

Any help from Marguerite would have to wait, because Bailey had given her housekeeper the next three months off and as a bonus paid for her tickets to visit her sister in New Mexico. She couldn't rescind that.

But suddenly she also couldn't help thinking that she didn't want to waste the next three months on a vacation. Not when she could spend them learning the ropes—as Jean put it—preparing herself for what she really wanted. For what she was determined to have.

Jean checked her watch. "We better get back."

But during the walk to the medical center and the rest of the afternoon's lectures, Bailey's mind wasn't on heart problems in obstetrical patients.

It was on canceling her trip and finding a way to get herself some mothering and household experience.

It might not have been how she'd intended to use this time. But the fact was, she had the next three months free, and Jean had just pointed out how she could better use it.

Chapter Two

The house was an older clapboard two-story with a big boxed-in front porch. It sat on a wide street—the kind built during the 1950s when homes weren't jammed together to get the most out of every inch of land. There was a strip of grass at the curb, then a sidewalk that stretched down the elm-and-oak-tree-lined street, then the front yard and the house set far enough back to be undisturbed by any car that came along.

The only thing Bailey was familiar with in Wheatridge—a suburb northwest of Denver—was Lutheran Hospital. When she'd talked to Gib Harden on the phone, she'd asked for directions to his place from there. And Saturday afternoon, instead of being on a plane bound for Africa, she pulled up in front of the butter yellow house trimmed and shuttered in pristine white.

It wasn't anything fancy, to be sure. But it was well taken care of—no chipped paint, no peeling gutters, and a yard that was neatly mown and edged even if it was littered with a red wagon, a tricycle, some fluorescent pink rollerskates, balls, a baseball bat and a number of other toys.

Bailey parked at the curb in front and checked the address on the slip of paper on her passenger seat. This was the place, all right.

She turned off her engine. Then she picked up the page from the classified ads section of the *Rocky Mountain News*—also on the passenger seat. It was folded into a square around the advertisement she'd circled. The advertisement that had led her here.

She read the piece again. For the umpteenth time since Wednesday when she'd found it.

Wanted: Live-in nanny and housekeeper for 3 kids and 4-bedroom home. No experience required. Desperate single father in immediate need of help.

That "no experience" was the most important part to her. A little on-the-job training was what Bailey had in mind. Similar to the last two years of medical school, when a good portion of a student's time is spent in the hospital, working with patients, learning through experience, in spite of the fact that they aren't doctors yet.

Since the medical conference and her conversation with Jean, Bailey hadn't been able to think about anything but how to get some lessons in housekeeping and child care. It wasn't as if there was a school for it, or she would have enrolled. And with Marguerite already gone, there was no hope for help from that front, either.

But thinking about Marguerite, Bailey had recalled that her fifty-year-old housekeeper had come to her in answer to a classified ad Bailey had run. That was when it occurred to her that if she answered one similar to that, she could get some experience herself.

Okay, so maybe whoever hired her wouldn't be getting the best end of the deal. At first, anyway. But this Gib Harden had it right there in print—''no experience required.'' And he was desperate. So clearly he wasn't looking for the cream of the crop.

She'd spoken with him on the phone on Wednesday evening, arranged for an interview and then spent the rest of the week trying to get comfortable with what she was about to do. Deceptions were not her style, and taking a job under false pretenses certainly qualified as that. But she just couldn't think of a better, quicker, more efficient way to accomplish what she needed to accomplish.

The week had also found her preoccupied, which was unusual for her. Preoccupied with wondering what kind of face went with the voice on the phone. A deep, rich baritone with an easy, smooth roll to it that made him sound calm, confident, patient, all-male and unwittingly sexier than any man had a right to be....

Not that those last two mattered. It was the other aspects of her telephone impression of him that were important. Positive aspects, Bailey thought. And not because his voice had washed through her like liquid heat. But because she hoped it meant he'd be good-natured, calm and patient with her while she got the hang of the job.

If she got the job.

Which was not going to happen if she stayed sitting in her car.

She checked her hair in the rearview mirror, brushed a single strand off the lapel of the cream-colored suit she'd chosen for the interview and finally got out.

The neighborhood was a nice, quiet one, so she didn't bother with the alarm on her dark green Jaguar. She just locked the doors.

Then she headed for the first three steps that climbed the upward slope from the sidewalk. She had to dodge a doll carriage that was abandoned on the cement walk that led to the house and a toy tank on the second set of stairs—four of them this time—to get up onto the porch.

More toys were scattered there, and she had to be careful about where she placed her feet all the way to the wooden screen. Standing open behind it was an old-fashioned carved-oak front door with an oval stained-glass center in the top half.

She couldn't see anyone inside, but she could hear a lot of noise. A baby crying. Other children bickering. A deep baritone ordering, "Share with your sister, Kyle," above it all.

She recognized the baritone as the voice from the phone call, and just the sound of it set off that liquid-heat feeling again. It struck Bailey as odd. An odd reaction for her to have to anything, let alone just the distant sound of a stranger's voice.

She decided to ignore it.

That wasn't altogether hard to do when she realized Gib Harden didn't sound so patient now, and she felt another pearl in the string of qualms she had about going through with this.

Ordinarily she was an honest, by-the-book kind of person. She was straightforward with her patients. She kept them informed about their condition, the progress of their babies to the best of her abilities to judge, good and bad. And even when she had bad news to tell someone, she tried to be as kind, as gentle, as compassionate as she could, but she never lied to them.

So she wasn't comfortable misleading anyone. But she could hardly tell the man who'd placed the ad the truth, either—that she wanted to use his house and family to learn from. He'd never hire her then.

Anyway, how hard could it be? she asked herself yet again—something she'd thought at least as many times as she'd read the ad. Teenagers baby-sat. If a thirteen-year-old could do temporary child care, certainly she could. And really that's all she'd be doing— the baby-sitting.

And some housekeeping. But everybody did that. Well, everybody but her. Still, what could it involve? Picking up a few things and putting them where they belonged, running a dust cloth over the tops of furniture, brushing out a toilet. No big deal.

If she got the job, she might be a little inept at first, but learning had always come quickly and easily for her. A day or two and she'd have things under control. And Gib Harden would never be the wiser. Then she'd give him and his kids a good three months of her best efforts before he'd have to place that ad again and look for someone new.

Not that she was going to tell him she'd only be there for three months—another of the things she'd omit. But she'd make it up to him. When it was all over with, she'd refund him every penny of the money he'd paid her, help him find someone to take her place, and of course she'd stay until he did so he wasn't left in the lurch.

That seemed like a fair exchange for her lessons in domestication and compensation for her subterfuge.

Since no one had happened by the open door to see her, Bailey rang the bell at exactly the same time that she heard something crash inside the house.

Louder wails were added to the din, these from an older child.

"We've got a mess up here, Gib!" a different male voice shouted.

Bailey couldn't be sure if the doorbell had even been heard. She hated to ring it again and insist on being attended to in the middle of what sounded like chaos. But she also hated to be late for her interview, to make a bad impression. And one glance at her watch told her she was right on the dot for her appointment.

So she rang the bell again.

"Hold on! I'll be right there!"

Gib Harden. He didn't sound calm, either.

Bailey stepped back from the door, wondering if she should sit on one of the wicker chairs on the porch and wait until things quieted down inside before pushing for this interview at all.

But just then a man who was a full ten inches taller than Bailey's five foot four appeared at the screen. "Yeah?" he demanded.

"Sorry to come at such a bad time," she said reflexively.

He stood there looking at her from beneath a questioning frown that pulled his full eyebrows nearly together over a nose that was just a tad long and slightly pointed at the tip. No kind of recognition whatsoever registered in his expression.

"I'm Bailey Coltrain? I spoke to Gib Harden on the phone Wednesday? We have an interview at one?"

Hazel eyes with bright green flecks in them widened, and he checked the watch that wrapped his thick wrist. "Is it one already? I didn't know it was so late."

He had on a plain white T-shirt that didn't look plain at all hugging broad shoulders and a chest so well muscled that it was hard to miss, even hidden by the knit and covered by the white shirt he had on over it. The shirt was open all the way down, the tails hung loose and the sleeves were rolled up to his elbows. He also wore old blue jeans tight enough not to dip lower than his waistline, even though he had a leather tool belt strapped around his hips.

Only the tool belt didn't have tools in it. Poking out of its pockets were a rag doll, an unused disposable diaper, baby powder, a travel package of wet wipes, a slingshot, some clean tissues, a lidded toddler's juice cup and a baby bottle.

Bailey fought a laugh at the sight it made. But it did strike her as funny. The man was big. Not just tall, but powerfully built. His wrists alone were the size of her ankles. His skin was a golden tan that spoke of work in the sunshine. There were faint lines fanning from the corners of his eyes, and his jaw was strong and firm and faintly shaded with what she had no doubt was a heavy beard that matched the bittersweet chocolate color of the thick hair that was cut short on the sides but left long enough on top to fall partway onto a wide, square forehead.

All in all, there was nothing about him that didn't shout rugged, pure, potent masculinity in a headturningly handsome package. Except for the contents of his tool belt.

He didn't seem to notice her struggle to keep a straight face as he pushed open the wooden screen door. "Come on in. I'm Gib Harden."

He stepped out of the doorway, and Bailey accepted the invitation, finding herself in a comfortable-size entryway, facing steep stairs directly ahead and a whole lot of mess in every direction she could see.

"I don't mind waiting, if you're not ready for me," she said, turning back to him.

He was still looking out the door, though. At her car. It hadn't occurred to her that people applying for work as housekeepers didn't ordinarily drive Jaguars, but she realized at that moment that it must have looked strange. She debated with herself about whether to lie and say she'd borrowed it if he asked.

She hadn't decided one way or another when he finally remembered her and turned to face her. Then he seemed to notice the clutter they were standing amid—toys, clothes, shoes, wet bathing suits, a half-eaten cookie and various other debris, some of it on the floor, some trailing up the steps, some in a path into the living room to the right of the entrance.

"You can see why I need a housekeeper" was all he said.

Another glance into the living room and Bailey thought maybe he needed a heavy-equipment operator and a bulldozer instead of a housekeeper. But she didn't say that.

Gib Harden stepped around her to the foot of the stairs and shouted up, "Jack? I've got the woman I'm supposed to interview for the job down here—"

"Hire her!"

"Can you handle things up there for a while?"

"Yeah, yeah. Go on."

Gib Harden aimed a long, thick index finger at a set of beautiful wooden sliding doors to the left of the entry. "We can go in there and talk," he said.

As he moved to them, he dug a key out of his pocket to unlock the brass lock that held them closed at their center meeting.

"This is my office at home. I have to keep it locked or I'd have peanut-butter-and-jelly-slathered blueprints," he explained, sliding the doors apart.

From the little Bailey had seen of the rest of the place she thought that anything that kept the room off limits was probably wise.

His manners were good. He waited for her to go ahead of him into a den that was paneled in dark wood. A barrister's desk took up one end of it, with a tufted leather chair behind it. In front of it were two smaller leather chairs, and against one wall was a matching sofa. Another wall held filing cabinets, and in the only remaining corner was a draftsman's table complete with stool and a library lamp attached to the side of it.

The sound of the doors sliding closed behind her made Bailey turn from her survey of the room to find him locking them in.

"I'm not trying to keep you prisoner. This is just the only way we'll be able to talk without interruption," he said. "My cousin is upstairs with the kids, but that doesn't mean any one of them—my cousin included—might not come screaming down here to get me to settle some dispute or another."

Bailey didn't doubt that. Not when she could hear all the yelling and crying that was going on upstairs.

As if he knew what she was thinking, he added, "All three kids have ear infections so they're unusually crabby."

Bailey nodded. *That* she understood.

"Let's sit down," he suggested, holding an arm out to the leather couch.

She sat in one corner of it, expecting him to go to the opposite end. But instead he took a manila file folder off his desk and then swung a chair from in front of it so he could sit facing her at a forty-five-degree angle, nearer than he would have been on the couch.

"Your résumé and reference letter came in the mail yesterday. Give me a minute to look over them and refresh my memory."

In the enclosed room, with Gib Harden only a scant few feet away, she was more aware of him as a man than she would have liked. Sunlight poured in from a large window and brought out auburn highlights in his hair. He held the file between the index and second fingers of massive hands. And she caught a faint whiff of a spicy after-shave that was almost heady.

Bailey reminded herself that she was here for a purpose—to gain some knowledge that would make her a better mother to a child of her own—not to get to know Gib Harden on any sort of personal level. Attractive though he might have been.

And he *was* attractive.

But she was enjoying the sight much too much.

In an effort to rein in her thoughts, she stared at the papers he was reading, mentally going over what was in them. She'd had her secretary write the reference letter but neither that nor her résumé held any mention of Bailey's real occupation. Instead they were both carefully vague while still giving unfounded assurances that she was a responsible, trustworthy person. All she could do was hope he accepted that without too many questions so she didn't have to lie too much more than she already had.

When he'd finished reading and glanced up from the file, he said, "Have you done this before? Been a nanny and housekeeper?"

"Not professionally," she answered, thinking that it was true enough, even if it was misleading.

"Are you married?"

"No."

"Do you have kids of your own?"

"No. I'm completely free and at your disposal." Had that sounded suggestive? She hadn't meant it to. But his presence seemed to fill the room so completely that she was having trouble ignoring it. More trouble not responding to it on some primitive level.

To compensate, she went on in a hurry. "I may be a little rusty at some things, but your ad did say no experience required."

"It did, didn't it?" And now he seemed to regret it. But he recovered quickly. "Let me tell you a little about what I need here. I'm on my own with three small kids—the youngest is twenty months, the oldest barely five. I own a construction company, and with building booming in Denver I have a full slate at work. I have to have someone to take care of the kids and cook and clean and do laundry and just about everything else around the house. I'm talking live-in help, being on the job twenty-four hours a day whether I'm home or not. And I might as well warn you upfront—

it's a demanding job. We've already gone through four housekeepers this year. When they quit they all said the same thing—they found out they couldn't have much life outside here."

Better that than they couldn't stand him or the kids, Bailey thought. But what she said was, "The hours are no problem."

"I can spare you on Sundays—that would be your only day off," he warned, as if she might not have understood him completely.

"Fine. But to tell you the truth, I don't even need that off." If she was going to get the full feel of what it was like to be a parent, she might as well stick to it seven days a week, the way the real thing would be.

"And the place has to be in better shape than it is now. *Much* better shape—it's a mess from top to bottom because I've been trying to work at home every minute the kids are asleep and chasing after them when they aren't. We don't need gourmet cooking, just good, wholesome food. Evie—she's the baby— needs to be toilet trained and switched over from the bottle to the cup full-time. Kyle will start kindergarten in the fall, so he'll need whatever it involves to get him registered and ready, and then he'll have to be driven to and from school. And shopping—grocery or otherwise—is in the job description—"

"In other words, everything a wife and mother would do, I'd be expected to do."

"Well, not everything a wife would do," he answered with just a hint of an upward twitch to one corner of his mouth.

From out of nowhere, completely uninvited, unwarranted and unwelcome, came a tingling in answer to what had only been a teasing insinuation, mingled with something else that felt like disappointment.

Odd. Very odd.

When Bailey recovered from her shock at herself, she slammed down on both the tingling and the disappointment and sat up straighter. "Of course," she said in a hurry, "I'll just need to do all the everyday things with the house and the kids—that's what I meant."

"Except on Sunday," he repeated. Now it was Gib Harden who seemed to be fighting a laugh. Probably at her obvious discomfort. Bailey could only hope he didn't know her discomfort wasn't over what she'd said but over what she'd felt.

"Really, I don't mind staying on Sunday," she said again to keep things going. "I won't have anything else to do."

That made him frown a little, and he seemed to study her more closely for a few moments. Then he set the file aside on an end table and relaxed back into his chair, bringing up an ankle to rest on his opposite knee. "Why don't you tell me about yourself."

For a moment Bailey's gaze stuck on those long legs—specifically on his thighs, which were big and hard and solidly encased in the worn denim of his jeans.

Then she caught herself and forced her eyes to his handsome face again.

"There isn't much to tell," she said, hoping it didn't sound as belated to him as it did to her. Or as false. "I'm a college graduate with a degree in chemistry. I was born and raised here in Denver. I don't have any family living. And I'd like to have this job."

"That's it?"

"I'm afraid so."

He studied her some more.

She fought the urge to squirm and felt as if he could see right through her, as if he knew her for the fraud she was. In this, if in nothing else she had ever done. At any moment he would call her bluff, she thought. And then what would she do? Besides die of embarrassment?

But he didn't call her bluff. He said, "If you have a degree in chemistry, why are you hiring out as a housekeeper?"

And so the lies get added to, she thought with a wave of guilt. "I've never used the degree," she said. *For anything except to get into medical school.*

"Why did you go for such a tough one if you weren't going to do anything with it?"

"I liked chemistry."

He seemed to wait for her to add to that. When she didn't, he went on watching her so intently that she thought she could feel his gaze on her. Not that it made her uncomfortable, strangely enough. Instead it was almost as if it exuded a warmth. An allure...

"There must be more you can tell me about yourself," he prompted, bringing her to her senses and leaving her wondering what had gotten into her.

"There just isn't more to tell. I'm a pretty quiet person. I've lived a pretty quiet life."

"Hobbies? Interests? Special talents?"

"I read a lot."

"What's your philosophy about rearing kids? Discipline, things like that?"

Good question. Too bad she didn't have an answer. At least not one that was her own. She did recall parts of what she'd been reading in parenting books since deciding to follow this course, so that was what she spouted.

"I believe in having a firm hand with a child where discipline is concerned. But I don't hit or condone hitting—not even spanking. I think positive reinforcement is the way to handle most things. Love and praise go a lot further than criticism does in teaching anything. I use time-outs for punishment and always try to reason with the child and understand what's causing the behavior. I think a well-balanced diet is best but wouldn't force a child to eat a food they didn't like. I'm not big on sweets but don't think an occasional treat will do any harm. Are those the kinds of things you mean?"

He nodded as if he approved but somehow knew she was just reciting things she'd read.

Or maybe that was just her conscience bothering her again.

"The pay is just average," he said then, but in a tone that still seemed to be testing her.

"I know. You told me about it on the phone," she said.

"Would you be willing to take a drug test and be fingerprinted?"

That surprised her. "I guess."

"My cousin Jack—" he pointed toward the ceiling in reference, apparently, to the Jack he'd hollered to upstairs before "—is a Denver police officer. He'll run the prints through the computer." It sounded like a warning.

But then who wouldn't be suspicious of a background and résumé as ambiguous as what she'd given him and an interview that wasn't any more candid?

"Fine," she answered.

"I'll know if you've ever had so much as a parking ticket."

"I haven't."

Once more he studied her, and Bailey knew he knew something was up with her. But this time she also knew he didn't know what it was.

He bent his head forward and scratched the back of his neck with one finger while still staring at her from beneath a brow that was wrinkled with uncertainty.

Then he said, "I'll be honest with you, Ms. Coltrain—"

"Bailey, please."

"Bailey. I'm having trouble getting someone who will take us on under these terms. So even though I wish you were more forthcoming with information about yourself, I consider myself a pretty good judge of character and I'm going to trust my instincts that you're just a private person and aren't hiding anything that would matter here. If you pass the drug test, don't have a police record and your reference checks out, I guess the job is yours."

"Great," she said without hesitation. Okay, so the house and three kids were somewhat daunting, but that made it all the better a lesson. Besides, the place was in such a mess she thought it would be hard to notice however inept she might be at first.

Actually, her biggest qualm was Gib Harden himself.

She wished she wasn't so aware of his attributes as a man, of the pure potency of his masculinity.

But how much would he be around? she reasoned. Not much, if he needed her to do everything.

And when he was home?

She'd just concentrate on the job and ignore him.

"How soon can we do the fingerprints and drug test?" she asked.

"Right now, if you have the time. My cousin can set it up—he's cashing in on some favors, so we can do it through the police department. If you can go from here to the station, we can get everything done today and have the results back by Monday. The sooner the better. I need someone to start ASAP."

"That works for me."

"Well, if you can head downtown then, I'll have Jack call so you'll be expected. His partner is a woman—Sergeant Marone. I understand she's catching up on some paperwork, but just ask for her and she'll take over from there. Then I'll be in touch on Monday."

For some reason that Bailey couldn't figure out, the anticipation of hearing from him gave her goose bumps. Again she squelched the odd rise of emotion.

"I'll be waiting to hear from you," she said, standing.

She caught him giving her the once-over from top to bottom—more the appraising glance a man gives a woman rather than the studying he'd done before. But he averted his eyes too soon for it to be obvious and stood to walk her out.

All the way out onto the porch, where he stayed watching her as she went to her car, got in and started the engine.

Bailey couldn't help sneaking a peek at him as she made a U-turn to leave in the direction she'd come in so she wouldn't get lost.

Gib Harden was leaning a shoulder against one of the porch posts, his arms were crossed over his chest, his weight was on his left hip, jutting the right out at an altogether too intriguing angle even with the tool belt hanging from it.

And on that handsome face was an expression of curiosity as he stared again at the Jaguar and then at her once more. He was curious and something else. Something that had renewed that tiny smile he'd shown her before when he'd assured her her responsibilities wouldn't extend to the romantic.

If circumstances had been different, she'd have thought he was interested in her. As more than a nanny and housekeeper. As a woman.

But that was crazy, she told herself as she lost sight of him in her rearview mirror.

She must just have been imagining it.

Chapter Three

Gib was at his desk at home at one o'clock Monday afternoon when the phone rang. As he reached for it, he hoped he'd remembered to turn off the extension upstairs. All three kids had been down for their naps for all of fifteen minutes, and if a scant fifteen minutes was the only peace and quiet he had today to work he was going to be up all night long finishing the estimate he had to have for his client the next day.

His second hope was that the caller was his cousin Jack with news about Bailey Coltrain. Good news about Bailey Coltrain.

The phone didn't have a chance to ring again before he picked up.

"Nanny investigations here," Jack said in answer to Gib's hello.

"Finally."

"Hey, you want speed, hire somebody else. How come it's so quiet there? You lock our little darlings in the closet?"

"Nap time."

"Hallelujah."

"Got that right."

"Are the kids feeling better?"

"Back to normal. No more fevers. Evie isn't crying constantly—she's just getting into everything again. Kate and Kyle are only fighting the way they usually do—over every other thing instead of over every single thing."

"And I'll bet you've been trying to work through it."

"Trying is the key word there."

"Hard to get anything done at home when they're sick, hard to get anything done at home when they feel all right—is that what you're telling me?"

"That's about it. So make my day and say I can hire my only nanny applicant who was over eighteen, under seventy, able-bodied, willing to take us on and didn't have terrifying ideas about what to do with kids."

"She also didn't have a police record like the last one you had me check out."

"No police record? Hallelujah," Gib echoed his cousin. "Does that mean I can hire—"

"The luscious Ms. Coltrain in the sparkling Jaguar? Yes, yes, please, yes." Jack had been spying from one of the upstairs windows on Saturday when Bailey had left.

"You haven't overlooked something you shouldn't have, just because you fell in love at first sight and can't wait to meet her, have you?" And why did his cousin's appreciation of the way Bailey Coltrain looked rub him the wrong way? Gib asked himself. Why should it bother him at all?

But it did. And it had been every time Jack brought it up. Which had been often since he'd had a look at her. If Gib didn't know better, he'd think the feeling was possessive. Jealous, even.

But how could that have been?

It couldn't. He just didn't want his cousin hitting on his kids' nanny. Distracting her. That was all.

"There was nothing to overlook," Jack said into Gib's thoughts.

"She's clean?"

"Squeaky. I ran her name and her prints through everything there is to run her through—locally and nationally. She doesn't have so much as a speeding ticket. Lab test showed no drugs, either. She's a gem."

"I don't think you can go that far just on a clear police record."

"A clear police record and my instincts."

"Instincts that kicked in just from looking at her through a window," Gib said dubiously.

"They're well honed."

Jack was only joking. But Gib couldn't find it funny. He had the strongest urge to tell his cousin to cool it. That Bailey Coltrain would be *his* house-keeper, and Jack had better keep his hands off.

He fought the urge. Not only because his cousin would think he was crazy but because he'd sound like Kyle or Kate squabbling over ownership of one of those action-figure dolls.

"I saw her first."

"But you didn't do anything with her and I want her."

"I want her!"

"She's mine!"

"No she's not, she's mine!"

Maybe he'd been around the house too much.

"Is the car registered to her?" Gib asked, forcing a strictly business tone to his voice and working hard to force any other thoughts out of his head.

"Yep, title and registration are hers and hers alone. And the address on both of those and on her driver's license is the same one she put on the application. So that chi-chi Cherry Creek residence is where she's lived for at least the past year since the license was renewed. Looks like you're getting an uptown nanny and housekeeper."

"She said she's never done this before professionally, but what if she wasn't telling me the truth about that. What if she worked there and got fired for some reason she didn't want known?"

"I can use the reverse directory and get you the name and phone number of whoever lives there, if you want to call and ask them."

"Do it. I don't want to take any chances."

"Hang on a sec."

Gib could hear a drawer being opened.

"Got the directory. Let me just . . ." Pages flipped. "Here it is. Nope. B. Coltrain is how the phone at that address is listed. It's her place."

"Nobody else there? A husband? No man's name at all?"

"Hey, you can't have her, so don't go getting interested in things like that. I want her." Apparently Jack had no problem sounding like one of the kids.

Gib just repeated his question. With exaggerated patience.

"Nope. No sign of a man's name at the address or on any of the car stuff. She looks to be on her own, driving snazzy wheels and living in the high-rent district. How about her reference? Did you check that out?"

"Yesterday. Woman said she's known Bailey very well for seven years now. Said she's a generous, fair, kind, compassionate, accomplished, intelligent person."

"In other words, she gave our Bailey a glowing recommendation."

Our Bailey. It really rubbed Gib the wrong way. He tried to ignore it.

"I'm not too sure glowing recommendations from references mean a lot. People don't give somebody as a reference if they're going to say lousy things about them. The woman did say she'd leave her kids with Bailey. If she had any kids."

"So are you going to hire her or not?"

"Doesn't seem to be a reason not to." Except maybe that she had eyes that were way too blue for his own good.

"Can I move in, then?" Another joke from Jack.

It irritated the hell out of Gib. "Ha, ha. Keep away from my help."

"You just want her yourself and won't admit it."

"You know better than that."

"I know, I know. You aren't interested in getting involved with anyone because you don't believe any woman really wants some other woman's three kids. And you worry that you don't give Kate, Kyle and Evie as much time and attention as you think you should, so you know you couldn't take on more kids that a woman might bring with her or want to have with you later on."

"Have I been boring you with that stuff?" he asked with a laugh, since his cousin had repeated his views to him with a note of impatience.

"No. I just think you're wrong all the way around. And wouldn't you know it—the one woman I could die for is the one woman who finally sparks your interest enough to tell me to keep away from her," Jack goaded again.

"I didn't say Bailey had sparked any interest in me. You just can't have her." Okay, so he could regress with the best of them. It seemed like a good time to get out of this. "I'll let you get to work, Jack."

"Yeah, sure. Ban me from the love of my life and then just hang up. What kind of cousin are you, anyway?"

"Thanks for the records check. I owe you one."

"One date with the nanny and we'll call it square."

"Bye, Jack."

Gib hung up and sat back in his chair, thinking about Bailey Coltrain. About her expensive car. Her high-priced address. The silk suit she'd worn Saturday. The precision haircut that left not a single strand of her shiny hair out of place, even when a toss of her head flipped it.

The whole picture spoke of money. Big bucks. And without a previous job to lay claim to.

Clearly she wasn't telling him everything. If Jack's investigation and his own conversation with Bailey's reference hadn't painted such a positive picture, Gib would have figured she was hiding something pretty negative. But as it was, another scenario began to take shape in his mind.

She might not have done child care or housekeeping professionally in the past, but just the way she'd
put that answer when he'd asked made him think she'd
done it before without being paid for it. Translation:
she'd come out of a marriage in which her husband
had been the breadwinner—a successful enough
breadwinner to provide all the perks of the car, the
elite address, the clothes—while she'd stayed at home
to keep house. Maybe there had even been stepkids in
the picture whom she'd helped raise.

But now she wasn't married. Maybe it had ended in
divorce. Maybe she'd been widowed. Either way, she'd
moved to her own place—paid for by settlement
money or maybe an inheritance.

But now some time had passed. Maybe she'd found
herself in need of making a living, or maybe just a
need to stay busy doing what she knows best and enjoys most.

In fact, when he remembered her reluctance to take
even Sundays off and her comment that she didn't
have anything else to do, that picture seemed all the
more likely.

And if her marriage had ended after a long time
with someone, she was probably still suffering that at-
odds feeling, not knowing what to do with herself,
with all the hours that had been so full before.

It was something he understood. Even with the kids
around and being buried in work, he'd felt some of it
himself after Angie had left.

Well, if Bailey Coltrain needed something to keep
her busy, Gib's house and his kids could certainly do
that for her. And in the process, he'd get what he
needed, too—an almost wife.

Not that he was painting her as anything but an employee, he reminded himself. Whether she was beautiful or not, that's all he had any intention for her to be.

But she was beautiful. With that skin that was so flawless it was nearly luminous. Those eyes that were wide and sparkling and as blue as a clear Colorado sky in the middle of summer. Hair that dark, dark brown and shining like polished wood. Soft, dusty-rose-colored lips that he'd had the urge to tease into a smile. And that small, perfect body with breasts just the right size to...

Gib pulled his thoughts up short.

What the hell was he doing thinking about Bailey Coltrain's breasts?

He didn't have any business doing that. And he didn't want to. He was hiring her to help out with the house and the kids, and that was all. The fact that she was easy on the eyes didn't make any difference. It was just a bonus. It didn't mean anything.

Except maybe that it would make it all the harder to keep Jack away from her.

And Gib really wanted to keep Jack away from her.

Not because he had any designs on her himself. Not because he was jealous. He couldn't possibly have been jealous.

But just because he wanted her concentrating on what he was hiring her for. It didn't have anything to do with wanting her all to himself. With wanting her at all. In any way. Except to clean house and watch the kids.

No, if Jack was in hot pursuit, he'd distract her and that was why Gib was against the idea of his cousin starting in with Bailey. That was all.

"And maybe if you work real hard, Harden, some-body'll believe that."

Gib Harden had called to formally hire Bailey at one-thirty that afternoon. Then he'd invited her to dinner to meet the kids and settle in.

So, with suitcase in hand, she arrived at seven o'clock Monday evening—the same time the pizza delivery boy did.

Following him up the walk, Bailey thought that she felt a sense of adventure every bit as strong as she would have had she been starting off on safari in Africa. It was like the first step on a path she was more eager to take than anything she'd ever done before.

This would prepare her for having a child of her own. For adding to a life that seemed only two-dimensional as it was now. The idea of getting to know some kids and what made them tick, learning the simple basics of taking care of them and of a house the way everyone else she knew did. Well, it was exciting.

And maybe some of the excitement was in seeing Gib Harden again, a niggling little inner voice said.

But Bailey didn't want to consider that, so she pushed it out of her mind. Just the way she'd pushed thoughts of Gib Harden out of her mind gazillions of times since she'd met him. Including as she'd stood at her dresser drawers, choosing what underwear to bring with her.

Seeing him up ahead, answering the door, made it more difficult to control her wayward mind, though.

Lord, the man was even better-looking than she re-membered. Tall, hard muscled, ruggedly handsome. His dark-chocolate-colored hair carelessly dusted his brow. He wore jeans again, and a shirt with the sleeves rolled to his elbows the way the white one had been on Saturday. But this time it was tucked into his jeans, buttoned down the front, and the light green shade accentuated the bright flecks in his eyes. Flecks that seemed to brighten even more when he caught sight of her behind the pizza boy and shot a quick once-over that took in her own blue jeans and plain tan camp shirt.

Having been paid, the pizza boy left and Gib Harden stepped out onto the porch with the two boxes braced on one upraised palm.

"Here, let me take your bag," he said, reaching for it with his free hand.

"That's all right. I can manage it."

But he took it, anyway.

"You can get the door," he suggested, since the screen had closed behind him when he'd come to meet her.

Bailey went around him and held it open again.

"Be prepared," he warned on the way in. "I've been swamped with work and kids, so I haven't touched the place."

To clean was what he meant. But Bailey would have known even without the warning. It wasn't as if the house was a health hazard of dirt and grime or smelled bad. It was just that everywhere the eye could see was the litter of kids—toys, clothes, pots and pans that looked as if they'd been played with, pillows and couch cushions dragged down, and all of it on top of what had been there on Saturday.

Gib set her suitcase in one of the few clear spots near the stairs. "We'll eat and get the kids to bed, then pick up some of this stuff while I show you around later."

He angled a strong chin up the steps that led to the second floor and raised his voice, "Kyle, Kate, Bailey and the pizzas are here. Come on down now." Then he led the way through the living room to the right of the entrance.

Bailey had some trouble navigating through the litter on the floor. It wouldn't have been so tough had her eyes behaved themselves and watched her step. But they kept straying and sticking like glue to the rear view she had of Gib Harden.

Broad shoulders and a very straight back formed a V to his narrow waist and a terrifically tight derriere.

And again Bailey had to consciously rein in her thoughts, reminding herself she wasn't there to notice things like that.

They went through a formal dining room that wasn't too messy; it merely held a flavored-crushed-ice machine on one end of a long oval table, cone-shaped papers and syrups here and there over the rest, plus a bucket of ice melting on the sideboard.

From there they stepped through an archway into a big country kitchen. Oak cupboards and redbrick walls gave it a cozy feel, along with the big round pedestal table in the center, surrounded by four spindle-back chairs and a highchair.

That room was an even bigger catastrophe than what she'd seen in the rest of the house. Dishes were piled in the sink, cooking and eating utensils—real and toy—were arrayed on the butcher's block countertops, more playthings were in clusters everywhere else and two of the lower cupboards spilled their contents in an avalanche of bakeware and plastic containers.

But she chose to overlook the clutter and focus on the baby sitting in the highchair, staring at her with the biggest green eyes Bailey had ever seen.

"Hello, there," she said in her best bedside-manner voice.

"That's Evie. Can you say hi, Evie?"

The tiny Evie just went on watching Bailey suspiciously, her fat-cheeked cherub's face devoid of reaction.

She had pale blond, downy hair that went every which way, as if she'd just gotten up from a nap and it hadn't been combed, and a Kewpie-doll mouth that opened only to put her lidded drinking cup into while she kept her gaze trained on Bailey.

"She doesn't talk much yet. And when she does, usually only Kate can understand any of it. Don't worry if you need her to translate," Gib said, just before he shouted, "Kate and Kyle! Dinner! Now!"

Bailey cringed slightly at the booming baritone.

Evie didn't bat an eye.

"I fed Evie her dinner already," he explained, as he tore the tops off the pizza boxes and placed them in the middle of the table that was set with four paper plates, napkins and plastic dinnerware. "Not enough clean dishes," he added then, apparently seeing her glance in that direction.

"Does Evie eat baby food or what everyone else does usually?" Bailey asked.

"What everyone else does. But spicy things tend to give her a rash—if she'll eat them at all—so I gave her noodle soup tonight. And bread and butter. She loves bread and butter. It just has to be cut up into real small pieces or she won't eat it. But then you must know that everything has to be cut up into real small pieces for a kid this age."

"It's better to be told what everybody's preferences are," she said, because it sounded better than saying she didn't *know* anything.

"What can I get you to drink? Milk, water, soda..."

"Water will be fine." She just hoped there was a clean glass. "But let me get it myself. You hired me to help, not to be waited on. And I might as well get acquainted with where things are." If they weren't in the sink, on the countertop or the floor.

He nodded over one shoulder. "Cupboard to the right of the sink. If you pour milk for the kids, too, I'll dish out their pizza."

"How about you?"

"I'll have water, too. Thanks."

Bailey found two tall glasses and two mugs with cartoon characters decorating them. Just enough for this meal and then the cupboard was bare.

About the time she had them filled and was carrying them precariously balanced to get all four to the table at once, two bolts of lightning in the form of small kids shot into the room.

"You're dumb."

"You're dumber."

"Am not."

"Are too."

"Cool it," Gib said in a firm tone. "I want to introduce you to Bailey."

The older of the two—the boy—glanced around the kitchen, passing Bailey up as if he were looking for someone else. When he didn't find anyone else, his gaze settled on her and registered surprise.

"Bailey? I thought that was a boy's name. But she's another *girl*."

"Mind your manners, Kyle." Gib again. To Bailey he said, "This is Kyle," and roughed up the little boy's blond hair.

It was shaved close on the sides, but about half an inch long on top, standing up like a bristle brush. His eyes were more the color of Gib's—hazel with green only in flecks. And he was missing his two front teeth.

Bailey set the glasses on the table, grateful she'd made it without colliding with either of the two kids. "Hi, Kyle. Nice to meet you. And I always thought Bailey sounded like a boy's name, too. But it's the only one I have."

"Don't you gots no middle name?" the little girl asked. "Like mine is called Ann. Kate...well, not jus' Kate...*Katherine* Ann."

"No, no middle name. Just Bailey."

"Do you want one? I'll think of it if you do." Kate again.

"*You* can't give her one," Kyle said, rolling his eyes in disgust.

"Can if I want."

"Can't neither."

"Can too."

"Okay, that's enough," Gib said. Then again to Bailey, he continued, "In case you hadn't guessed, this ragamuffin is Kate."

She was a ragamuffin, too. It looked as if she'd dressed herself and combed her own darker blond shade of hair. The ponytail was askew and there were more strands outside the rubber band than inside it. She had on red striped shorts and a maroon-colored polka-dot T-shirt over which she had about a dozen beaded necklaces in a rainbow of shades. She was a cute little girl, though, with the same big green eyes and chubby cheeks as Evie's.

"I got no teeth," Kyle offered then. "Kate knocked 'em out with a baseball bat."

"Accidentally," Gib put in.

"I'm four," Kate said, holding up the requisite fingers and pushing them at Bailey three times. "Four yearses old. I'm four yearses old."

"She's three and eleven months," Gib confided in an aside.

Kate ignored him. "How many birsdays old are you?"

"Thirty-five," Bailey answered, picking up the cup Evie had thrown on the floor and then demanded back with a pointed finger and a pretty clear "Mine!"

"*Thirty-five?* Tha's *old.*"

"Climb up into your chair and eat your pizza, Kate," Gib said with a note of exasperation.

Bailey wasn't insulted. She just laughed. "At not quite four, I guess thirty-five does sound ancient."

"That's not so old," Kyle offered in Bailey's defense. "Uncle Gib's thirty-seven. That's older."

Uncle Gib?

No one but Bailey seemed to find that odd. Instead, he nodded at her chair and said, "Go ahead and sit down."

And before she had a chance to ask about the title, dinner started with a bang.

Kyle wanted the cheese off his pizza but the olives put back once it was.

Kate wanted hers cut into pieces she could eat by stabbing them with a toothpick rather than a fork.

Evie kept throwing her cup on the floor so some-one would pick it up.

Kyle spilled his milk.

Kate wanted a second glass. Then, as she reached for it, she knocked her plate into her lap.

And all the while Kate and Kyle lobbed one question after another, showed off and bickered between themselves every step of the way.

It was impossible, in all the noise and mayhem, for Bailey and Gib to have any conversation at all, let alone for her to ask why these kids called him *Uncle Gib*. It was almost next to impossible to eat.

Then Evie started to cry for no reason Bailey could see, Kyle hit Kate and made her cry, too, and over the din, Gib said, "Welcome to my madhouse."

"It isn't always like this," she said hopefully.

"It isn't?"

"Is it?"

He shrugged one of those broad shoulders. "Now you know why I need help."

She knew, all right.

She just didn't know how much help she'd be.

Especially when she lunged to catch Evie's cup, hit her own glass of water with her elbow and knocked it into one of the pizza boxes, flooding what was left of that pie and making an even bigger mess than anything the kids had made.

Bath time came right after dinner, before any kind of kitchen cleanup got under way because it was getting late and the kids were increasingly grumpy.

"From here on, if you plan dinner for about six, the evenings will go a little better," Gib instructed.

Planned dinner. Bailey had a wave of panic at that thought. But with tonight's meal just finished, to-morrow night's seemed far enough away not to dwell on it.

The upstairs level of the house held four bed-rooms, each with its own private bath—something Gib explained he'd remodeled the second floor to pro-vide. Evie and Kate shared one room, Kyle had his own, Gib's was the master suite and he pointed to the remaining closed door to let Bailey know the guest room would be hers.

But he didn't pause to show it to her. They'd get to that later. Instead he was more intent on juggling Evie, her bedtime bottle and the rag doll she wouldn't let go of, while trying to direct Bailey to the linen closet for towels and wash cloths.

"Uncle Gib?" Kyle whispered.

"Don't interrupt," Gib said in the middle of telling Bailey how often laundry needed to be done.

"Uncle Gib?" Kyle whispered again, anyway.

This time Gib ignored him, finished his laundry lecture and then both he and Bailey turned to the lit-tle boy.

Kyle gave Bailey a sideways glance, turned his head in the opposite direction and spoke from the corner of his mouth, "She can't come in while I take my bath."

"It's okay," Gib assured him, nodding as one man to another. "I'll come in to finish you up." Then to Bailey he said, "Kyle bathes himself, but he has to have the tub filled for him and if somebody doesn't check to make sure, nothing above water level gets clean. But that'll be my job. The girls can share a bath as long as one of them isn't too dirty and you—"

Before he could tell her to do it on her own while he saw to Kyle, Bailey said, "Why don't I just observe tonight so I'll know just how they like it from here on?"

"It isn't complicated."

It was for someone who'd never done it before. "Still, everybody will feel better if I know how to do things the way they're used to," she reiterated.

A small frown pulled Gib's brow, but he didn't press the point.

Baths and bedtime routines took an hour and a half, even with Gib trying to hurry things along. Bailey watched closely, learning how to bathe the kids but interested, too, in Gib himself.

She couldn't help being impressed by him. As a father, he was patient, kind, loving, and he seemed to get a kick out of his young family, despite the work and chaos and commotion and mess that swirled around everything they did. He dug right in, got down on his knees beside the bathtub to scrub little bodies, wrapped the girls in towels and ignored the water they splashed all over him, pulled the baby onto his lap to make sure she was good and dry before diapering her and slipping her pajamas on.

With Kyle he used a man-to-man attitude that made the small boy cooperate more easily than he might have, had he just been ordered to do what needed to be done.

And through it all, Bailey couldn't help being aware of just how much man Gib was. Of that great derriere jutting out as he bent over the bathtub. Of those big hands gently tending to tiny ears and cupping the baby's bottom when he hoisted Evie out of the water, or roughing up Kyle's hair to praise him for not hitting Kate back when she hit him first. Of his broad chest when Evie laid her weary little head against it on the way to her crib.

It had never occurred to Bailey before that watching a man take care of children could be sexy. But it was. *He* was.

"Will you be heres tomorrow when we wake up, Bailey?" a sleepy Kate asked after Gib had finally tucked her in.

"Yes, I will be."

"Can you make pancakes for bres'fast?"

Uh-oh. Looked as if she didn't have until dinner to worry about cooking.

But Gib unwittingly saved the day. "I think we'll have to wait for pancakes until Bailey gets things organized around here."

"The nextest day, then?"

"We'll see. Just go to sleep now," Gib whispered, kissing the little girl's forehead and then straightening up to aim a long, thick index finger toward the door for Bailey to go out ahead of him.

He turned off the light and followed her into the hall. "Listen to that," he whispered.

"I don't hear anything," Bailey whispered back, fighting the sense of intimacy that seemed to have formed around them all on its own.

"That's the point—it's quiet. Enjoy it when you can get it."

She was enjoying something, all right. But it was less the peace and quiet and more the man.

She watched him take a deep breath that expanded his chest, and into her mind popped the idea of placing just one palm there to see if it was as hard as it looked.

Then he exhaled and she reprimanded herself for the inappropriate thought.

"Well, on to kitchen duty," he said.

And a good thing, too. Better that she concentrate on the job she'd been hired to do than on the man who had hired her.

Since she knew her way around now, Gib held out an arm, motioning for her to go ahead of him back downstairs.

Also better, she thought, because that way she wasn't ogling him from behind again.

The kitchen was no less disastrous than it had been when they'd left it. "Too bad," she said as they went into it. "I was hoping little elves might have come in to clean up while we were gone."

"The only little elves around here are the ones who *make* the messes."

Bailey didn't have any idea where to start or what to do, but once more Gib stepped in before that could become too obvious. "Why don't you clear the table while I start rinsing what's in the sink and loading the dishwasher?"

"Okay."

Not such a tough task. Bailey tossed paper plates into the pizza box she hadn't spilled water into, on top of what was left of the pizza.

"We should put the food down the disposal," he said when he saw what she was doing. "Although you could have saved it and given it to the kids for lunch tomorrow."

"Oh. Sure." Bailey felt like an idiot having to be told that. To cover up—and to soothe her own curiosity—she said, "Why are you *Uncle Gib* instead of Dad?"

He turned on the water and started work on the stack of plates, pots, pans, silverware and glasses. "Because I'm not Dad. Well, biologically, anyway. The kids are my nieces and nephew. Their father was my brother."

"Was?"

"He and my sister-in-law were killed in a car accident about a year and a half ago."

"I'm sorry."

"It was pretty bad. A huge shock. One minute they were here, dropping off the kids for an evening. The next minute someone was on the phone saying they were dead. Didn't seem real. Sometimes it still doesn't."

"And a night of baby-sitting turned into raising three kids?"

He laughed, not heartily but it was a warm chuckle rumbling out of his throat. "That's one way of putting it. But no, I didn't end up with the kids by default. My brother and his wife had had a will drawn up just after Evie was born—two months before the accident. They came to me, said in the event both of them should die, they'd like it if I'd raise the kids and would I be willing to do that. I said I would."

"But people say things like that without thinking it will ever really happen."

"You got that right."

"Only this time it happened. Were you okay with that?"

"Well . . ." He seemed to think about it, remembering maybe, chuckling again. "It wasn't as if I—we—I was married at the time—weren't brought up short by the reality. My brother and sister-in-law were dead. My family was in a tailspin. And here were three kids—

one of them only two months old—who were going to need to be *raised*. Long term. A lifetime commitment to kids I—we—hadn't planned. At a time that wasn't altogether opportune. Was I okay with it? Not overnight, no."

"But?"

"I was crazy about the kids themselves—don't get me wrong. But being crazy about them as their uncle is not the same as being a parent to them. It's a whole lot different, in fact. On the other hand, I'd told my brother I would do it. I'd made him a promise, essentially, and even if I hadn't believed I'd ever have to make good on it, it was still a promise. So the kids became mine."

"Wow. That's a big undertaking."

"I'm not sorry. Once I got over the shock and really accepted the idea, it was definitely okay. And then it was good. I wouldn't have it any other way. I just need some help with it all."

It was on the tip of Bailey's tongue to ask what had happened to the woman he was married to at the time, but that seemed too personal. If he'd wanted to say, he would have.

"And there you have it—my rapid road to fatherhood," he said, dampening a sponge and handing it to her when she'd put all the paper products from their dinner in the trash. "You can wash off the table and the countertops. I'll get the dishwasher started. Tomorrow you can deal with the toys and the stuff Evie dragged out of the cupboards and get the rest of the things in here put away. I'm sure you'd like to get settled in now, and I need to finish the estimate I've been trying to work up all day."

Bailey did as she was told, even more impressed with her new boss than she had been before for keeping his word and taking on a job as daunting as raising three kids who didn't belong to him.

"What else is on the agenda for tomorrow?" she asked to distract herself again.

"I'm off to work early. Don't worry about my breakfast—I can fend for myself. You'll just have to deal with the kids and the house. I'll be home between five and six, but if you need me during the day I can be reached at one of the numbers there on the chalkboard next to the phone."

Bailey glanced up to see what he was talking about.

"That leaves you on your own," he continued. "I'll let you make up whatever schedule suits you, as far as that goes. Cleaning, cooking, what we talked about that needs to be done around here. Let's hold off a day or two on starting Evie's toilet training, until she gets used to you. Other than that, it's just full speed ahead—whip this place into shape and take care of the kids."

Just like that.

But looking around, Bailey realized they'd made a big improvement in the kitchen already. With a whole day ahead of her, she shouldn't have any problems with the rest of the place.

"What time do the kids wake up in the morning?"

"Whenever. They're not late sleepers. Sometimes before I leave for work, but not always. They'll let you know when they're ready to start the day, believe me."

He shined the faucet and handles before folding the dish towel he'd used and putting it away, as well as Bailey's sponge. Then he turned to face her, crossed

his arms over his chest and smiled. A charmingly dev-
ilish smile. The first he'd directed at her.

"So. Are you in? Or have we scared you off just in
the past few hours and you're planning to sneak away
in the middle of the night?"

She smiled back, secretly basking in the warmth of
his expression. "I don't think I'm ready to go sneaking off into the night, no."

"Good. I'm glad to hear it. I'd hate to have that
happen."

Was she imagining it, or was there an undertone of
something personal in that? Could he have been flirting with her just a little?

No, she had to be mistaken, she told herself.

"Come on. I'll show you your room," he said then,
laying a hand against her back only briefly to pivot her
toward the door.

It was a small thing. Friendly. Courteous. But it sent
ripples of delight from the spot where his hand met her
spine, all the way through her. And worse yet, when
he took it away, she felt a wave of disappointment.

Make sense of that! she told herself, thinking that
no medical book she'd ever read had explained such
intense physical reaction to anything so inconsequen-
tial.

Again she led the way, retracing their steps through
the dining room, living room and entranceway, where
Gib picked up her suitcase.

"Don't be shy about using anything around here,"
he said as they climbed the stairs. "There's a VCR on
top of the television, the stereo is on one of the shelves
of the bookcase—if you hadn't noticed. Feel free to
bring in any of your own things—just be warned that
once they're here, they're in jeopardy from kid dam-

age. Oh, and I have a key for you to use to get into my office. You may want to duck in there for a minute or so periodically to save your sanity."

They were at the top of the steps by then. Bailey reached for the key he'd taken from his shirt pocket to hold out to her, barely brushing her fingers against his as she took it. But it was enough to set off more of those ripples from his touch.

She withdrew her hand in a hurry, wondering if there was just a lot of static electricity in this house and that's what she was feeling.

Gib opened the door to the guest room and waited for her to go in.

It was a room the size of the kids', large enough for a double bed, a tall bureau, a dressing table with a mirror, a closet that would only take up a corner in her own at home and a small bathroom with a full-length mirror on the door that connected it.

The walls were the same cream color as the rest of the house, the carpet was the same tan shade and there was a fairly big window that looked out over the front yard.

All in all, it was nice. Homey. Pleasant. Clean. And the bed, with its navy blue quilt and four fluffy pillows, looked inviting.

Bailey had no problem with it as her home away from home for the next three months.

What she did have a problem with was the thought that her evening with Gib was about to end.

"There are towels and washcloths in the vanity under the sink. Soap in the medicine chest..." he was saying, oblivious, she knew, to what she was thinking.

And what she was thinking was that if the evening they'd just spent together had been a date, she would have judged it a great success.

But thoughts like that were out of line. Almost as out of line as the other thought that crept in—that successful dates usually ended in good-night kisses...

Lord. What was wrong with her? She had to remember that she was here for lessons she could use when she went back to her own life. Lessons in housekeeping. In child care. It didn't have anything to do with this man.

"If you need anything you can't find, just holler. For now I guess I'd better get downstairs and go to work."

That registered more than the rest of what he'd been saying—he was leaving.

Bailey's first inclination was to do something to stop him, to keep him there and prolong her time with him.

But she didn't. She wouldn't. She controlled herself.

"I'll be fine, thanks. Don't let me keep you."

Still though, he didn't grab that opportunity and run with it the way he might have. Instead he stayed standing there in the center of the room, glancing around as if he might have been as reluctant to leave as she was to have him go. As if maybe he'd enjoyed her company as much as she'd enjoyed his.

Then he seemed to pull himself together.

"Okay. Well, if I'm out of here before the kids get you up in the morning, I guess I won't see you until I get home tomorrow evening. But I'll probably call during the day to make sure you're doing all right."

"Okay."

"I suppose that's about it. I can't think of anything else I need to tell you so I'll just say good-night."

"Good night."

With no reason to stay, he headed for the door.

Bailey watched him go, watched him pause in the hallway just outside her room, cast her a small parting smile before he reached back in and closed the door between them.

And she surprised herself one more time when she realized she was hoping the kids did wake her up early. No matter how early, so long as it was before Gib went to work.

Because she wasn't sure she could wait through the whole next day until the evening to see him again.

Chapter Four

Bailey had her alarm set for six the next morning. Time enough, she thought, to get up, take a shower, comb her hair and dress before the kids woke up.

And maybe also time enough to sneak in a few minutes with Gib before he left.

Not that she admitted openly even to herself that wanting those few minutes with him was the main reason she was willing to get out of bed at the crack of dawn.

But it was.

Setting her alarm didn't matter, though. Before it ever went off, she came out of a deep sleep to a child's voice whispering, "*You* wake her up."

"No, *you* do it."

"No, yoooo."

It took Bailey a moment to remember where she was and put names to the whispers.

"I think she's dead," Kyle said. "Lookit how her mouth's open."

"Everybody sleeps with their mouthses open," Kate answered.

"But she's not makin' no noises like Uncle Gib does. I can't even hear her breathe or nothin'."

There was an edge of concern to Kyle's voice, so Bailey opened her eyes.

Standing at the side of her bed, not a foot from her face, were the two small kids, studying her as if she were Gulliver and they were Lilliputians.

Even with her eyes open and staring back at them, they still didn't budge, as if they weren't sure what it meant.

Kyle wore the pajamas he'd put on after his bath the night before, but Kate was dressed. Green shorts, purple T-shirt—inside out—necklaces, bracelets and red rain galoshes. And her hair was in another ponytail, this one on the top front of her head, bobbing down over one eye, and again with more strands straggling than caught in the rubber band.

"Good morning," Bailey greeted the two of them.

Kate jabbed her brother. "I knewed she wasn't dead!" Then to Bailey she said, "Misser Moose comed over today and he wants bres'fast."

Mr. Moose?

Bailey looked beyond the kids to see if someone else was with them. No one was. More likely whoever Mr. Moose was, he was waiting downstairs. For her to prepare breakfast.

Great. A guest for the first meal she'd ever been responsible for providing. She felt a rush of adrenaline that matched her first emergency as a medical student.

Not the way she'd wanted to start the day. Especially when Gib was probably downstairs with their guest and she'd have to see him before she'd done anything to make herself presentable.

But there wasn't much she could do about it, she decided. He hadn't hired her to look good—he'd hired her to work for him doing things like getting breakfast when breakfast needed to be gotten.

She sat up in a hurry. "Just let me throw on my sweatsuit and I'll be down. Tell your da...uncle Gib and Mr. Moose it won't take me five minutes." During which time she hoped she could figure out what to fix beyond cold cereal and milk. Even her coffee wasn't usually anything to brag about.

"Uncle Gib's not with Mr. Moose," Kyle said, as if Bailey were out of her mind. "Uncle Gib a'ready goed to work."

Maybe it was later than she thought. Maybe she'd slept through her alarm. After all, she had had trouble falling asleep the night before with all those crazy thoughts about Gib being just downstairs, then just next door, getting ready for bed, going to bed...

It had been after two before she'd finally gone to sleep.

Bailey took a quick glance at her alarm clock: 5:54 a.m.

Why had he left so early?

"You guys go and keep Mr. Moose company until I get there. Can you do that?" she said to the kids.

"Kate can. Not me," Kyle said.

"Just hurry. Misser Moose is *hungry*," Kate put in, and the two of them left the room.

Bailey did a mad dash for the connecting bathroom, wondering as she threw herself into a barely presentable state who this Mr. Moose was and if Gib had known he was coming for breakfast and forgotten to tell her, forgotten even to stay himself.

And what was she going to serve? Toast? She could make toast. Maybe he wouldn't want more than that. Maybe she could claim there wasn't anything but toast and dry cereal in the house because she hadn't shopped yet. That might work. Especially with Gib already gone. And disappointed as she was that she wouldn't get to see him, at least there was the advantage of not having any impromptu cooking giving her away so early in the game.

Then it occurred to her that maybe Mr. Moose was someone Gib worked with. That maybe the man had come by to have breakfast with Gib before they went to work and Gib had gone out for doughnuts. That he'd be back in just a few minutes. That maybe the kids were alarming her for nothing and she'd be spared having to feed anyone. And that she'd get to see Gib, after all.

With the last swipes of the brush through her hair, she heard Evie's first stirrings and fast on that an "Up!" issued from the girls' room.

Taking care of the baby didn't seem like something Bailey could postpone.

She went out of her own room to the top of the stairs and called down, "I'm sorry to keep you waiting, Mr. Moose, but Evie's awake now, too. Let me just get her up and I'll be right there."

No response. But she could hear the sounds of the television, so at least the kids were entertaining him. Not worrying about it, she did a run-walk to where Evie's "Up!" was sounding more insistent.

Bailey had every intention of just grabbing the little girl out of the crib to bring with her downstairs. But Evie had taken off her pajamas and was in the process of stepping out of a very wet diaper when Bailey got there.

"Hi!" the tiny child greeted her, holding the drenched disposable diaper out to her as if it were a gift. Then she went on to garble words Bailey couldn't understand at all. But she didn't want to call Kate upstairs to translate, so she just took Evie out of the crib, laid her on the changing table she was getting too big for and put on a fresh diaper. Not adeptly, but it was on.

Finding clothes took a while longer, not only because Bailey had to go through drawers and decide which things were more Kate's size than Evie's but also because she knew better than to leave Evie on the changing table. Yet she couldn't set the little girl down—every time she did, Evie made a run for the door. So she was left having to carry the baby *and* search the drawers.

Then, when Bailey finally located a pink flowered playsuit, she had to wrestle with the squirming child who did not want to be dressed at all.

A full half hour had passed by the time she actually got downstairs. Kate and Kyle were in the living room, at the coffee table in front of the TV, eating cookies. But no one else was in sight.

"Where's Mr. Moose?" Bailey asked.

Kyle didn't look up from the cartoons he was watching.

"Here," Kate answered, pointing to the spot beside her where someone had stepped on cookies and ground them into the carpet.

"Did he go into the kitchen for something?" Bailey tried again.

"No. He's he-yere," Kate insisted.

Something about this didn't fit. "Who *is* Mr. Moose, Kate?"

"My frien'."

"Not your uncle Gib's friend? Or somebody Uncle Gib works with?"

"No. Just my frien'."

Kyle finally looked away from the cartoons. "Nobody but Kate can see 'im."

Ah, Mr. Moose was an *imaginary* friend.

"He likeded the cookies but he wants pancakes for bres'fast."

Bailey didn't know whether to laugh or cry.

She laughed, albeit wearily, and was grateful Gib hadn't been there to see her rushing around to serve a breakfast she couldn't prepare to an imaginary moose. Even if it did mean she'd missed seeing him altogether.

So there she was, at barely past six-thirty in the morning, alone with three hungry kids and in need of starting the job she'd taken on.

Now or never, she told herself. *Get with it.*

"No more cookies for anybody," she decreed, taking the package with her free hand—the other arm held a wiggling Evie on her hip. "Let's go into the kitchen."

A trail of cookies marked the way, as if whoever had brought them out hadn't realized they were falling from the bag. After Bailey stepped on one herself, she was more careful about where she walked. Until she actually got to the kitchen. Then shock set in.

Two kids alone for half an hour had destroyed what little order Gib and Bailey had managed the night before.

The refrigerator was open, an orange juice carton had turned over and juice spilled down the front of the shelves, baptizing everything along the way and leaving a puddle on the floor.

The pantry door was open, too, and looked as if a burglar had done a fast search through it.

Drawers were gaping.

The trash had been overturned to dump what appeared to be traces of Gib's breakfast—wet grounds for coffee and a half-eaten muffin complete with crumbs.

And the spray nozzle on the sink was stretched as far as it would go, hanging out over the counter's edge like a panting dog's tongue and leaving another puddle on the floor.

"Misser Moose has to drink from the hose," Kate explained when Bailey replaced the spray nozzle.

And thus began her day.

For every mess she cleaned up, one or more of the kids made a new mess. For every toy she put away, at least two others appeared. While she straightened out the upper shelves of the pantry, Evie emptied the lower ones. When she tried to put the bakeware and plastic containers back in the cupboards from which they'd sprung, Evie threw a fit and pitched it all out again.

Kate and Kyle fought and flung things at each other like ground-to-air missiles. Or they played together, dragging couch cushions onto the floor and pillows and blankets from the upstairs linen closet to build a fort in the living room.

Evie dirtied her pants. While Bailey changed her, Kate gave Mr. Moose another drink of water and flooded the kitchen again.

Kyle took out his army to play war and set up the battlefield on the dining room table around the crushed-ice debris Bailey didn't have time to pick up. A gazillion small plastic men, tanks and planes joined the clutter, on a field of sand he brought in from outside when Bailey wasn't looking.

Kids, Bailey began to think, were a little like cockroaches—everywhere and into everything.

And she was no help to herself.

It was Bailey who spilled Evie's bowl of soup at lunch as she tried to do too many things at once. Bailey who didn't know how to assemble the pieces of the vacuum cleaner and instead had to handpick cookie crumbs out of the carpet on her hands and knees while Kyle tried to ride her back. Bailey who was inept at diaper changes and ended up sticking her elbow in Evie's mess. Bailey who sopped up spilled orange juice but, in her hurry, dripped almost as much on her way between the refrigerator and the sink to rinse the sponge.

By nap time at one o'clock, she still hadn't spent so much as a moment on herself. The house was an even bigger disaster than it had been the night before, and she was ready to beg for Marguerite's help. If Marguerite had been anywhere within begging distance. But she wasn't.

Bailey was on her own.

That thought and plain old weariness deflated her onto the bottom steps of the staircase on her way from having put the kids to bed for their naps.

She felt awful. Not only tired and discouraged but grimy. One o'clock in the afternoon and she hadn't had a shower, hadn't brushed her teeth. Lord, this was as bad as internship.

But then that's what it was, wasn't it? Her first day of internship as a care-giver and housekeeper.

No wonder she was so lousy at it. The first day was never good.

And that thought gave her hope.

She'd ended up being a good intern. A better resident. An even better doctor. The first day was not an indication that she couldn't do this. It was just the first day.

And the best way to feel as if she had some control over the situation was to get things accomplished now that she was free of the kids for a few hours.

Which left her with the choice of what to do—see to herself and then clean? Or clean and then see to herself?

As she considered it, her gaze drifted to the hall tree beside the front door. Hanging there was the tool belt loaded with kid paraphernalia that Gib had worn on Saturday when she'd arrived for her interview.

That one glance was all it took to conjure a picture of him in her head. Of the way he'd looked with that tool belt slung low on his hips.

And it set off a fluttering in her stomach. The same fluttering that had come spontaneously every time she'd happened across something in the house that reminded her of him.

Silly things. His coffee mug in the dishwasher had made her think about his mouth, wonder if it was as soft as it looked when he talked, when he grinned. His jackets and coats in the coat closet reminded her of his broad shoulders, the span of his chest. Even just walking past his bedroom door or the door to his office had caused everything else she should have been thinking about to be blocked by the image of the man.

There was something about him that she just couldn't get out of her mind. A lot of men had crossed her path in thirty-five years of life—relatives, friends, more than friends—but no one had ever lingered around the edges of all her thoughts this way before, ready at the drop of a hat to slide into mental view and capable of causing a reaction with nothing more than that.

It was strange.

But then, he was more man than she usually encountered. More muscular. More charming. More good-looking. More easy natured and patient and compassionate. More down-to-earth. More potently attractive. To her, at least, when the simple flicker of his smile could turn up the thermostat inside her.

It was almost as if he had some sort of power over her thoughts. Over her. Power enough to keep her up half the night listening for him. Imagining him standing behind his desk downstairs, those big hands splayed on either side of a blueprint to hold it down, thick wrists—thicker arms—bracing his weight as he leaned over it, that clean bittersweet-chocolate-colored hair falling across his brow.

Power enough to imagine him climbing the stairs when that sound had reached her, to see those hard thighs lifting him closer, closer to where she was. Power enough to leave her wondering if those wonderful hazel eyes had drifted to her door on the way to his, if he was thinking at all about her when she couldn't stop thinking about him.

And then there had been the sounds of him going to bed. The wondering what he wore, if maybe he didn't wear anything at all. What he looked like in the buff...

She had to stop this, she told herself. Just the way she'd told herself a hundred times last night. She couldn't live in the same house with him—working *for* him—and be thinking the things she was thinking.

She had to curb it. Concentrate on the kids. The house.

And she meant it, too.

Except when she thought about using the only free time she might have to either clean or go upstairs and whip herself into better shape before Gib got home, she just couldn't make herself spend that time cleaning. Even if it meant the house might be the same wreck when he got there that it was at that moment.

"Just a quick shower, a quick shampoo, a quick brush of mascara, a little blush," she whispered to herself as she stood and climbed back up the steps.

There were two main objectives in hiring a nanny and housekeeper: to bring some order to the home front and to free Gib to work.

As he sat in his office at Harden Construction, he trusted that Bailey Coltrain was bringing order to the home front. But she was sure as hell not freeing him to work. Because even though he'd gotten away from the house and kids, he still couldn't keep his focus on nuts and bolts. Only now it wasn't the house and kids distracting him. It was Bailey Coltrain.

She was the reason he hadn't finished up the estimate last night. The reason he'd had trouble going to sleep. Staying asleep. The reason he'd ended up out of bed this morning at five.

He'd spent the remainder of the past evening thinking of two dozen other things he could tell her about the house, the kids. Nothing important. Just things that would be an excuse for him to draw her out of her room so he could see her once more. He'd even headed for the stairs when he should have been working, only to fight the urge at the last minute and make himself go back to his desk. Four times. Until he'd finally given up trying to work at all.

Then he'd climbed the stairs, wondering the whole way if he could knock on her bedroom door and say a second good-night without looking like an idiot.

He'd fought that urge, too.

But lying in bed had been the worst.

He'd started picturing her in *her* bed so nearby. That silky hair against the pillow. Those long, dark eyelashes dusting her cheeks, heavy with sleep. Her lips parted, soft, relaxed, inviting. A sheer, lacy, sexy nighty barely covering that small, perfect body...

Torture. That's what it had been. That's what it still was. A ton of work to do—work he'd put off in the past two weeks since the last nanny quit—and instead of doing it, he was daydreaming about the new nanny.

When he'd interviewed Bailey, he hadn't realized how attracted he was to her. Okay, so he'd realized he might have been. But he'd pushed it aside. It wasn't important. He could ignore it. He needed help with the house and the kids and if she was willing to do it and fit the bill, that was all that mattered.

He'd never expected her to be as bright as she was. As articulate. As easy to be with. He sure as hell had never expected to enjoy the time they spent together as much as he had. To feel as if it was over long before he wanted it to be. To drive himself crazy trying to get it started again.

But there it was. All true. Every bit of it. He hadn't felt that way about any woman since his divorce. Even about terrific women he'd met, dated, liked.

But none of them had stuck in his mind the way this one had. Or stirred up what this one had.

And this one wasn't someone he was dating or could pursue for a personal relationship. He hadn't hired her to play house, and by God he wasn't going to let that happen.

He wasn't going to give in to the attraction. That was all there was to it.

In fact, to prove it, he ought to call Jack and invite him over to meet Bailey, let his cousin start something up with her.

He thought about Bailey with Jack. Jack smiling at her, teasing her, making her laugh. Jack putting an arm around her straight back, a hand at one of her small shoulders. Jack pulling her into an embrace, pressing that great body against him. Jack kissing her...

Gib's fists curled into tight knots. His jaw locked. He broke out into a sweat. He wanted to hit something. Somebody. Jack.

For nothing, he reminded himself, shocked at his own response to what was no more than fantasy. It hadn't really happened anywhere but in his head. Bailey didn't even know Jack existed.

And that's how he wanted to keep it.

No way was he going to call his cousin and give him the go-ahead with her. No way was he going to let Jack anywhere near Bailey.

He'd just have to deal with the attraction. With the thoughts of her. The craving for more time with her. For more of her. He'd just have to deal with it all on his own. Quietly. Firmly. And without his cousin horning in.

But it wasn't going to be easy.

It wasn't going to be easy at all.

It was going to be damn tough.

Because the truth was that he'd only felt this way once before in his life, about one other woman. Angie.

"And look how *that* turned out," he reminded himself aloud.

So maybe he *should* give Jack a chance with Bailey before he got himself an emotional punch in the gut like that had been.

No, he absolutely would not let anything personal or romantic develop between himself and Bailey Coltrain, no matter how she'd captured his interest or his imagination.

But he sure as hell wouldn't let Jack enjoy what he was denying himself, either.

It was incredible to Bailey that kids could get up so early in the morning, nap for barely an hour and still have as much energy as Kate, Kyle and Evie did.

More incredible still that that single hour when they'd napped had gone so fast.

Then there they'd been again—rarin' to go, to make more messes where even they hadn't made messes before.

And by five-thirty that afternoon, tallying up what she'd accomplished as she carried Evie downstairs from another diaper change, Bailey was not awed by her day's work.

Oh, sure, the beds were made now and she had showered, brushed her teeth, put on a dab of makeup, combed her hair and dressed in her best white shorts and red camp shirt, but as far as anything in the whole house looking better? Nothing did.

In fact, there were things that looked worse.

The living room was torn apart with Kate and Kyle's tent of couch cushions, pillows, blankets and toys. The dining room still looked like a sandbox battle site with a crushed-ice concession stand. And Evie had emptied a third cupboard, this one of pots and pans, to go with the bakeware, plastic containers and foodstuff from the pantry.

It wasn't as if Bailey hadn't tried—hard—to get more done. It was just that she was outnumbered and faced with so many already existing messes along with the new additions, she was doing all she could to keep up with those things in need of immediate attention.

Plus it didn't help that she didn't know what she was doing. That she had no organization. No plan. No method. No control over the kids...

The first day, she reminded herself. *This is just the first day. I'll do better tomorrow.*

She went through the dining room, hoping for some sort of bolt of lightning to strike about dinner before Gib got home. When she hit the kitchen she found Kate squirting water into midair, flooding the floor for the fourth time today.

"Oh no, Kate, not again," Bailey moaned.

"Katherine Ann! You stop that now! You know better than that!"

Bailey jumped a foot at the roar of Gib's baritone voice from the back door. She hadn't seen him there, only one cowboy-booted foot over the threshold.

"Misser Moose needs a drink," Kate answered, undisturbed by her uncle's tone.

"Mr. Moose drinks outside, not from the kitchen spray," he told her in no uncertain terms. "Now go in the other room."

Bailey felt as if she'd been caught in the act of something she was doing wrong herself and forced a small smile. "Hi. I didn't know you were home."

But then he just barely was as he stepped the rest of the way in before he could close the door behind himself.

And even through her own chagrin and his frowning entrance, Bailey couldn't help noticing how ruggedly good-looking he was in his low-riding jeans and madras-plaid shirt.

"I take it you know about Mr. Moose?" she asked then, not wanting to stare.

"Kate's imaginary friend. Yeah, I know about him. I should have warned you. He's a good excuse for her to do a lot of things she knows she's not supposed to."

"Like playing with the spray nozzle on the sink."

"Like playing with the spray nozzle on the sink," he confirmed.

The kitchen seemed to catch his attention then. Actually, the disarray of the kitchen seemed to catch his attention, and his gaze did a slow roll from the sight of one disaster to another, his green-flecked eyes widening more and more as he went along.

Bailey waited for him to lower the boom. To explode. Maybe to fire her on the spot.

But he looked more dumbfounded than anything, and what he chose to comment on surprised her.

"You haven't started dinner yet?"

Either, she thought he probably wanted to add but didn't.

Thinking fast, she said, "If we order in again, it'll be my treat since my first day wasn't very productive. And while I wait for delivery, maybe Evie won't notice me straightening the cupboards and the pantry again and I can actually get it done—I've been trying all day but she drags everything out faster than I can put it away."

"Sit her in her highchair with some graham crackers," he suggested.

"And order dinner?" Bailey said hopefully.

"I need to shower. You could throw something together while I do that."

"Really, I'd like to buy dinner. I didn't get around to even thinking about anything to cook."

His eyebrows took a brief hike toward his hairline at the admission of that, but still he didn't comment. "Okay. I guess another night won't hurt anything."

"Great! What is there around here that delivers? Besides the pizza place from last night?"

He suggested a Chinese restaurant, told her where to find the phone number and what he and the kids liked, all the while stealing glances at the room around them as if he couldn't quite believe his eyes.

Just wait until you see the rest of the house, Bailey kept thinking, but she pretended not to notice that they were standing in a circle of evidence that she didn't know what she was doing.

Then Gib walked out of the kitchen and found the battle site in the dining room. Bailey saw him pause, shake his head, then move on to the demolished living room and pause again.

And somehow she knew that even though he hadn't said anything about what he'd come home to, the jig was up and he was rapidly figuring out just what a fraud she was.

Still, hoping to regain some ground while Gib showered, she placed the order for dinner, set Evie in the highchair with crackers and juice and went to work on the kitchen.

The first order of business was to dry up Mr. Moose's most recent drinking hole. The pantry got second attention and then the cupboards—all at a breakneck speed to redeem herself, with little thought to doing it well or neatly, just jamming everything out of sight as fast as she could.

Unfortunately, about the time she closed the cupboard doors on her efforts, she turned to find that rather than eating the graham crackers, Evie had broken them into pieces and crumbs all over the highchair's tray, poured juice into the mix and smeared the resulting glop in her hair, on her face, down the front of her and across the back of the kitchen chair that was within her reach.

"Oh, Evie," she moaned yet again.

Before Bailey could even begin to clean up the little girl, the doorbell rang, so she left Evie as she was and headed for the entranceway, intending to tell the delivery person to wait just a minute while she ran to her room for her purse.

But Gib beat her to it and was paying the man when she got there.

"This is my treat," she insisted.

Gib took the bags of food and closed the door. "Paying to feed my family is not your responsibility."

But she'd done such an abysmal job with what was her responsibility that she would have felt better if he'd have let her pay. Especially when she led the way back to the kitchen and the mess Evie had made because Bailey hadn't been watching her.

"I had my back turned," she said, when Gib first laid eyes on the baby, hating the need for yet another excuse but not knowing what else to say.

"It's okay," Gib answered.

But he sounded disappointed, and the whole time he was wiping off Evie's face his brow was knitted together into a frown.

Bailey could almost hear his thoughts. Anyone who knew what she was doing would have at least made a dent in the work that needed to be done around here. She wouldn't have left the place in worse shape. And she would have kept a closer eye on Evie. On all the kids, for that matter, so they didn't make mud out of graham crackers to smear all over themselves, so they didn't tear apart the living room, burglarize the pantry, bury the dining room in sand, flood the kitchen floor...

Oh yeah, the jig was up, all right.

Dinner was as chaotic as it had been the night before, so again Bailey and Gib didn't get much talking done. But Bailey kept feeling his eyes on her, and she knew he was looking for more signs of her ineptitude.

Afterward, while Gib did Kyle's bath, Bailey managed to give Kate and Evie theirs, drying the floor with the girls' towels before Gib could see how much she'd slopped over the side.

Then, when he gathered all the kids onto Kyle's bed to read them a bedtime story, Bailey went back to the kitchen to finish cleaning up the dinner mess on her own.

She was going to have to say something to him about how bad she was at what he'd hired her for, she decided as she emptied left-over Chinese food from the cartons it had come in. She just hoped that if she offered him enough assurances that she'd work hard and learn to do a better job of it, he wouldn't fire her.

She turned on the disposal at the same time she used a fork to poke chow mein down the drain. Too far down because the disposal suddenly yanked the utensil out of her hand, pulling it in with a terrible clatter-bang-clatter-bang.

That brought her out of her thoughts with a panicked rush of adrenaline.

She could see about half an inch of the end of the handle going round and round just above the guard. Maybe enough to grab...

"No! Turn it off first!"

Gib's loud baritone shout from the doorway behind her startled her for the second time that evening, and she pulled her hand back as if she'd been bitten.

Turning off the disposal hadn't occurred to her in her panic. But that's what she did. In a hurry to stop the noise. Then she retrieved the mangled fork.

"I'm sorry," she said, holding it up.

Gib didn't say anything. He just came to stand beside her and switched the disposal on again. When it roared to life, he said, "No harm done. It's still working. The fork doesn't matter." Then he shut off the disposal once more. "I'll finish up here. Why don't you wipe down the counters, the table and Evie's chair?"

In other words, why didn't she do something where she couldn't harm anything.

Bailey didn't balk at the suggestion. She dampened the sponge and got out of his way.

"Are the kids asleep?" she asked, just to make conversation while she tried to figure out how to begin her confession.

"They're out like lights," Gib answered. Then, after a moment's hesitation, he said, "So, do you want to tell me about how your day went?"

It was a leading question, and she doubted she'd find a better segue, so she decided to use it. "Not tremendously well, as you can probably tell."

"Not a lot got done, I can tell that. But from hearing Kate and Kyle talk, it wasn't as if you sat around all day."

"No, I definitely didn't do that."

"The kids said it took you a long time to figure out how to put on Evie's diaper, and that you didn't know how to hook up the hose and nozzle on the vacuum cleaner, so you had to clean cookie crumbs off the carpet on your hands and knees, and—"

Bailey got the picture. "I've been squealed on."

"Sounds—and looks—like you don't know what you're doing around here. Am I wrong?" he asked kindly.

She appreciated that kindness more than he could have known. Another man might have raged at her, demanded explanations, ordered her out of his house. And Bailey thought she deserved no less.

But instead he just seemed curious and concerned.

"No, you're not wrong. I'm in a little over my head." And maybe not just with the kids and house. Maybe with him, too, she thought as she glanced at him washing out the sink, shining the faucet, and found herself thinking what an attractive sight he made even doing that.

He'd changed into another pair of jeans—these with frayed holes at the knees that somehow seemed more sexy than ragged to her, and a plain white T-shirt that cupped his muscular chest and back, and stretched taut across the bulge of his biceps. His hair glistened clean and he'd shaved the shadow of beard he'd come in with earlier, so the sharp line of his jaw looked smooth and smelled of clear spring air.

He sighed, gave a small laugh and then glanced at her over his shoulder. "It isn't only that you haven't done nannying and housekeeping professionally, is it? You haven't done it at all."

"No, I haven't." She finished with the sponge, brought it to him, and while he put it away, she said, "I've always had help around the house myself."

He turned toward her, leaning a hip against the counter's edge and bracing his weight on one hand that rode the tap. "How much help have you had?"

"Today was the first time I ever made a bed."

"You're kidding."

"I'm afraid not."

"How is that possible?"

"I told you, I've always had help around the house."

"Even as a kid, you never had to make your bed?"

"No."

He closed his eyes and scrunched up his face as if he'd just heard a bad joke. "It's worse than I thought."

"How bad did you think it was?"

"The car, the clothes, the address, no previous employment—I figured you'd been married to a man with money, been a housewife, maybe had stepchildren you'd taken care of some—"

"No. I've never been married. Never been around kids."

"You don't even have any practical knowledge—is that it?"

"None to speak of. But your ad said no experience was required," she reminded him.

"It didn't occur to me that that opened the door to someone who'd never even made a bed before."

It seemed wiser to put a positive spin on this than to dwell on the negative. "I'm a quick study. I'll learn before you know it and be a whirlwind. Honestly. If you'll only be a little patient with me while I get the hang of it."

He closed his eyes again, shook his head. And laughed. A full, big, barrel-chested laugh.

Bailey thought it was a good time to keep the ball rolling. "I just need to get the hang of things. But I want this job more than you know. I like the kids . . ." *And you. Maybe too much . . .* "If you'll just bear with me, give me a chance . . ."

What he gave her was the once-over when he opened his eyes, lingering slightly at her legs below her shorts before meeting her gaze once more. "Let me just understand this completely. You don't know *anything* about cooking? About cleaning? About kids?"

"I know what I've learned in the past twenty-four hours," she said with a smile, because he didn't look daunting standing there, staring at her. His expression was calm, maybe even amused, not foreboding at all.

"Only what you've learned in the past twenty-four hours," he repeated, as if he still couldn't believe what he was hearing.

"I can do this, Gib. I can." It was the first time she'd said his name, and she liked the way it felt on her tongue, liked the sound of it in her own voice.

"You know, I'm really in a bind," he said. "I need the help. And I don't have any more time to spend trying to find somebody to do this job. But—"

"I can do it," she said again with enough enthusiasm to mask her own doubts.

"You really need the work?"

"I do," she lied. Fudged, actually. It was just a matter of semantics. She might not have needed the work, but she definitely needed the experience that came with it. In fact, after a single day she realized Jean had been right, that having a child of her own was more involved than just getting pregnant. A lot more involved. And that she'd better learn the ropes before she did it because there were so many ropes to learn.

Gib was standing there, debating with himself. Or at least that's what Bailey thought he was doing.

It occurred to her that she should sweeten the pot while she could. "You can dock my salary for anything I ruin—like the fork. And pay me less until I get up to speed, if you want."

"It isn't money or things getting ruined. There's the kids—"

"Graham crackers in the hair, water on the floor, sand on the dining room table—those things aren't dangerous. I didn't even let them play outside today because I hadn't okayed it with you first—Kyle snuck out to get the pail of sand when I wasn't looking. But if I erred with the kids it was on the side of overprotectiveness. I'll make absolutely certain they're well looked after.''

Still he stared at her, but Bailey thought she detected a warmth in his eyes that meant she was winning the battle.

"Come on," she urged, "let's go put the living room back together and you can think about it."

He still only stared at her out of the corner of his eye for a moment before pointing his strong chin toward the other room to let her know he was agreeing to her suggestion. But just to her suggestion to straighten out the living room. He clearly wasn't conceding to anything else.

"So where are you really coming from, Bailey?" he asked as he followed her lead.

She recited her address.

"That's not what I mean. Being my housekeeper and nanny won't cover the payments on that Jaguar you have parked out front."

"It's paid for," she said. "It was a gift from my parents for my thirty-third birthday." Which was true.

"Uh-huh. You've never made a bed before—even as a kid—and your folks gave you a Jaguar for your birthday. Do you want this job to get a taste of how the other half lives? Is that it?"

She didn't like the sound of that. It wasn't as if she came from some upper-crust, life-of-leisure background. She came from people whose prosperity was the result of hard work and long hours. She'd worked long and hard herself. Just not at household kinds of things.

"I haven't lived in the lap of luxury. It's only that what I've done hasn't included cooking, cleaning or child care. But I've come to a point in my life where those are things I want to know how to do, too."

"So what else *have* you done?"

Treacherous waters. Bailey stacked the pillows the kids had brought down from upstairs on the coffee table Gib had just put back in its rightful place.

"My family emphasized education. I have a lot of it. But that's the trouble now—I'm long on academics and short on life experience."

"And you want us to give you a crash course in those life experiences."

"On-the-job training. If you'll let me keep the job." She caught him looking at her legs again with what seemed like an appreciative glance.

But then he averted his eyes as if resisting the influence of anything he liked about her.

All that was left to do with the living room was fold the blankets Kate and Kyle had also dragged down from the linen closet. Gib handed Bailey an end of one and stepped back with the opposite end.

"Take a chance on me," she urged, not intending to flirt but somehow hearing it in her voice, anyway, as they stepped together, drew back, stepped together again to fold the blanket.

"I don't like that you weren't straight with me from the start," he said, but with the exception of one eyebrow raised at her, he didn't seem too seriously upset with her.

"I'm sorry. But you wouldn't have hired me if I'd told you I'd never done this before."

"No, I probably wouldn't have."

"Even though your ad did say no experience required."

"You're not going to let me live that down, are you?"

"And what it boils down to is that I'm here now. All moved in. Why not let me stay? See if I don't prove to be just what you need, given a little time?"

He did the last fold by himself and set the blanket on top of the pillows. Then he handed her her end of the second one. "Just what I need, huh?" he said, more to himself than to her and in a way that sounded as if it had some meaning she hadn't intended.

He watched her, holding her eyes with his as they did the minuet with that blanket, too, drawing near, parting, drawing near once more.

He appeared to be thinking everything over. His expression was serious, and it seemed to Bailey that with each coming together this time, they ended up closer than the one before. Or was she imagining it?

And how could something as mundane as folding a blanket give her such a thrill?

Then Gib stepped near again to take the last edges all to himself the way he had before. Only when he did, his hands closed over hers and held them while his eyes seemed to draw her in, searching hers as if he could find the answers to all his questions by just looking deeply enough into her face.

Bailey met him eye-to-eye, losing herself in the hazel-and-green-flecked brilliance of his, breathing in the scent of his after-shave, feeling the warmth of his big body infuse her.

Was his handsome face coming nearer to hers? Slowly, slowly nearer?

It crossed her mind to wonder if he was going to kiss her.

But that was crazy, she told herself. He was unhappy with her. With what she'd disclosed to him.

Wasn't he?

And then all at once the distance between them widened.

"I'm in a bind," he repeated, but in a deep, quiet voice that almost sounded intimate. "Or I'd kick you out on your ear, *Ms. Coltrain.*"

Bailey kept on looking up into those green-flecked eyes of his, still close even if not as close as they'd been moments before. "Does that mean you *won't* kick me out on my ear?"

He seemed to think some more about that as he studied her face, frowning at her.

"I guess it does," he finally said a little gruffly, only then retreating with the blanket and putting more distance between them than he needed to accomplish that last fold. Then he grabbed up the pillows and blankets in one swipe, holding them pressed to his chest as if he needed the physical barrier to keep himself away from her.

But even with his arms full, he managed to poke a long index finger at her. "But you better catch on real quick," he warned.

"I will."

He didn't say any more. He just went around her and climbed the stairs.

She listened to each step, realizing her heartbeat was keeping pace, wondering if he'd come back down again. If he'd really almost kissed her or if she'd only imagined it.

But he didn't come back. She heard the linen closet door open and close. Then what sounded like his bedroom door open and close, too.

But it was better that he didn't come back, she told herself. And better that he hadn't kissed her, too, if that's what had been on his mind. Better that this had stayed a purely working relationship, even if it was a somewhat grudging working relationship now.

The only trouble was, she didn't feel better.

She was still not being completely open and honest with him, and she was sorry for that.

But she'd gotten what she wanted, and she tried to take some comfort in it. She wanted to stay, to go on with what she'd started here.

And if she'd also wanted him to go through with that kiss that might have been?

It served her right to be left unsatisfied on at least that front.

Chapter Five

Gib wondered if he was doing the right thing about Bailey when he opened the pantry door at five-thirty the next morning and most of what was in it avalanched out. How wise was it to have a housekeeper he had to clean up after?

It wasn't too late to terminate her employment, he told himself. He could make coffee, sit and have a cup until Bailey came down, then tell her he'd slept on the idea of her staying and decided against it. After that, he'd just have to place another ad for another nanny-housekeeper and start the interviews over again until he found one. One who had some experience.

But even as he replaced the contents of the pantry, Gib knew he wasn't going to do any of that.

He didn't want to go through interview after interview again. He didn't want—and couldn't afford—to miss more work staying home while he did.

But the real reason, when he got down to it, was that he didn't want to fire Bailey. Not just because he didn't want to look into those big blue eyes of hers and say, You're fired. But because he didn't want her to go.

He was keeping a housekeeper who couldn't keep house because he liked her too much to lose her.

Now that was some convoluted thinking.

But it was the truth, and as much as he wished he could deny it, he couldn't.

Especially not when he remembered that coming home to her yesterday had had him speeding because he could hardly wait to get here. And once he'd made it and gotten past Kate's squirting water onto the kitchen floor, he'd been focused so intently on Bailey that he hadn't initially even noticed the other messes in the kitchen. Instead he'd been aware of the race of his own pulse the minute he'd laid eyes on her in that bright red shirt, those shorts that showed her long, beautifully shaped legs. Nothing else had even registered. For a moment, anyway.

And how much effect had those legs had on his decision? he asked himself now. Because great legs were hardly a testament to her abilities. Was he doing the kids potential harm by leaving them in her care?

The house was one thing—little by little, working together, he and Bailey could probably get it under control and he could teach her what to do along the way. But the kids were something else entirely.

He blocked the vision of her legs out of his mind and forced himself to be objective. The question was, Were Kyle, Kate and Evie safe with her?

But thinking about it he realized that nothing had happened to lead him to believe they weren't. They'd gotten into mischief, but they got into mischief no matter who was with them. And really, from the kids' reports, a good part of the reason Bailey had accomplished so few things around the house was that she'd spent most of her time trying to meet the needs of one or the other of the kids.

Better that than the way it had been with other women who had preceded her and kept the house immaculate at the expense of looking after the kids.

No, Bailey might not be adept at the job he'd hired her for, but she wasn't negligent, either. And the kids seemed to like her, which was also something that couldn't be said of some of those who'd come before her. Plus he *was* back at work....

The coffeemaker had stopped dripping by the time he finished the pantry, and he poured himself a cup, leaning against the edge of the counter, staring into space while in his mind's eye he pictured Bailey again.

"Admit it," he ordered himself quietly. "You just don't want her to go."

And he didn't. In fact, he didn't want her to go so much that as long as he felt sure the kids were okay with her, he didn't mind the thought of a messy house he needed to pitch in to help clean. Because he'd be pitching in beside Bailey and it gave him an excuse to spend that time with her.

Wouldn't Jack have a heyday with that bit of information!

On the other hand, Gib thought to make himself feel better, Bailey was sharp, bright, energetic—she probably *would* catch on to things around here in a hurry. There was no reason not to give her the benefit of the doubt and a little leeway to learn.

Except of course that she hadn't been honest with him during their interview. And she was still not free with much information about herself or where she'd come from or what she'd done before this, so she could well have been lying to him about her intent to get the hang of this job he'd hired her to do, too.

Yet somehow his instincts about her still made him inclined to give her that benefit of the doubt. To stick with his decision to let her have the chance she'd asked for.

Because if she did what she said she was going to and learned the job, he'd end up with just what he needed in the way of a housekeeper and nanny, and still have her to come home to.

And *that* was worth a little patience and extra effort on his part. For a while, anyway.

He just wouldn't let Jack know that there was an outside chance he was letting himself be duped because he was so attracted to Bailey Coltrain that he couldn't seem to do anything else.

Bailey had started the day determined for it to be better than the one before.

It just didn't happen.

Oh, she managed not to stick her elbow in dirty-diaper mess and didn't let Kate soak the kitchen floor or Kyle bring sand into the house. But she also didn't accomplish much more than immediate maintenance for the new catastrophes they whipped up. Unlike the previous day, Gib wouldn't come home to anything worse than he'd left. But he wouldn't come home to anything better, either.

Even the fact that she let the kids play outside some of the time because Gib had left her a note telling her they were okay in the backyard as long as she kept an eye on them wasn't much of a help. There was just so much to do with them whether they were inside or not.

Noses had to be wiped. Faces and hands had to be washed. Meals and snacks had to be served then cleaned up after. Disputes had to be mediated. Endless questions had to be answered. Drinks of water, milk and juice had to be dispensed. Wrongs righted. Broken things fixed. Diapers changed. Problems solved. Needs met. One after another, after another.

Bailey was beginning to think Gib should hire four people—a separate caretaker for each child and the fourth to actually clean the house.

At five that afternoon, the sand, soldiers and crushed-ice-machine menagerie were still in place in the dining room. Toys, dust and litter still cluttered the place in general. The bathrooms were still a disgrace. And the cupboards she'd jammed things into to get them out of sight still hadn't been straightened and were likely to spill their contents with no more encouragement than opening the cupboard door. But by then Bailey knew better than to think she was going to conquer any of it yet today, and since cooking was a high priority, she turned her thoughts to that.

At home Marguerite always had something in the refrigerator that Bailey could heat and eat. Or she went out. Or ordered in. Food was something she ate, not something she prepared.

But how hard could it actually be? She'd gotten A's in chemistry. If she could do that, surely she could make hamburgers or a casserole or something. It was basically the same principle, wasn't it? It was all a matter of how she looked at what was in the refrigerator, the freezer, the pantry. She had to see them as parts of a whole she could put together instead of something ready to eat without any effort.

She stood with the pantry door open. Then with the refrigerator door open. Then with the freezer door open.

Then she decided to call Jean.

Jean wasn't a great cook, but she at least knew her way around a kitchen.

Jean's last appointment of the day was never scheduled past two-thirty so she could be out of the office by three-thirty to deal with her own kids after school. Bailey knew her friend's home number by heart and dialed it, stretching the cord far enough to be able to see Evie, Kate and Kyle through the window over the sink while she talked.

All looked peaceful enough for the moment. Kate was swinging on the swingset and singing at the top of her lungs. Kyle was throwing a spongy basketball into a low, freestanding hoop, and Evie was in the playpen in the shade of a big elm tree, poking different-shaped blocks into a cube with holes to match each one.

Jean picked up on the third ring.

In answer to her hello, Bailey said, "Whatever you do in the next ten minutes, don't say I told you so."

It only took a split second for Jean to realize who she was. "Is this Bailey Coltrain calling me from the safari into the suburbs?"

"Very funny."

"How's it going?"

"I managed not to lose the job last night. Of course tonight might be another story."

Jean laughed. "Got your hands full, huh?"

"You might say that."

"And are you calling for help or just to chat? Because if it's just to chat, I need to warn you I only have a few minutes before Kristy is due at soccer practice and it would be better to talk later."

"I'm calling for help." Although Bailey hated to admit it. "Just a little. What are we having for dinner?"

"Here, we're having pizza delivered—soccer practice gets over too late for me to cook."

"Had that the night before last. And Chinese delivered last night."

"In other words, you've dodged the cooking bullet twice and tonight had better fix something."

"Right."

"But you don't have the slightest idea what."

"Right again. I thought maybe you could talk me through something. But since you're short of time, maybe you could just point me in a direction I can follow on my own?"

"What are the possibilities?"

"You mean, what is there to cook?" Bailey took a parting glance at the kids, then moved back to the pantry, refrigerator and freezer, reciting the contents to her friend.

"Sounds like the cupboard is pretty bare, Mother Hubbard. Spaghetti is probably your best bet. Open that jar of sauce, doctor it up with some fresh garlic or garlic powder or garlic salt—depending on what you have—and basil, oregano, thyme. Add small amounts, taste it, add more if it needs it and simmer it awhile. Then boil spaghetti and put them together. Did I hear lettuce on the list of what's in the fridge?"

"No. No lettuce. Just some carrots."

"No salad, then. Bread? Canned veggies?"

"Sliced bread. Cans of peas, corn, green beans—"

"Any white cheese—provolone, mozzarella, Parmesan, Romano?"

"Parmesan."

"Jazz up the sliced bread with some cheese, some of whatever kind of garlic you have, parsley, maybe slices of fresh tomato if you have one. Toast it till the cheese melts. Open any one of the veggies and voilà! Dinner."

None of that sounded difficult. "Great. You're a lifesaver."

"So tell me in two minutes or less what's happening there. Are you doing all right with the kids? The house? The dad?"

"Two minutes isn't even a start. Suffice it to say that Gib—the man I work for—is letting me stay out of necessity and the kindness of his heart. As of last night, a lesser man would have throttled me."

"So you like him?"

"I like him. He's great, actually."

"Great as a boss? Great as a man? Great as a man you could have a close personal relationship with..."

All of the above. But Bailey didn't want to admit it. Even to herself. "He's just a really nice boss."

"Young? Good-looking?"

"Thirty-seven. No slouch. Not that the way he looks makes any difference in the world." But it didn't do any harm that he was easy on the eyes.

"Didn't you say he does something in construction? I'm guessing tan, built, earthily handsome?"

That about summed it up. "Don't you have to go now?"

"He must be cute or you wouldn't be dodging my questions. Any sparks flying between the two of you?"

Did imagining him on the verge of kissing her when they were folding blankets count as sparks? "I'm just lucky he didn't ask me to leave when he came home yesterday and found the kitchen floor flooded and sand dunes in the dining room."

"*Sand dunes* in the dining room?"

"You don't want to know."

"And I don't have time to or I'd badger you into telling me. About the sand dunes *and* the man."

"But you don't have time. Thanks for the dinner ideas. I'll talk to you soon," Bailey said, getting off before Jean could delve any deeper into territory Bailey was trying not to think about.

Evie started to cry then for no reason Bailey could see through the window, and she figured her grace period of peace had ended. She went outside to get the baby, and both Kate and Kyle followed her back in.

"I'm gonna teach Evie how to color in the color book," Kate announced. Then, as she took a box of crayons and the coloring book out of a drawer, she added, "Kyle gots a mouse in his pants and he used Uncle Gib's toothbrush to wash 'im."

"A mouse in his pants?" Bailey repeated, not sure she was understanding what the little girl was saying.

But Kyle stared daggers at his sister, so she knew something was up.

"What mouse?" she asked him.

"The one he catchded by the garage to scare me with," Kate again.

"What mouse, Kyle?"

"You'll be scared, too."

"I won't be scared. What mouse, Kyle?"

"This one," he said, pulling the small gray animal out of the pocket of his shorts.

Bailey's first thought was of the diseases a field mouse could carry. With that in mind, she quickly grabbed a pair of rubber gloves from under the kitchen sink, put them on and held out one hand, palm up.

"Give him to me. You can't just catch a mouse and keep it in your pocket or in the house without a cage."

"But yer a *girl*. Girls can't hold mouses."

"It wouldn't be the first time. Just give him to me."

Kyle's mouth opened into a wide oval of surprise as he set the mouse in her gloved palm and she didn't do anything but cup her hand around it and pet its head with her other index finger.

"The mouse didn't bite you, did it?" she asked, again thinking about the dangers of the tiny rodent, though she felt reasonably sure Kyle wouldn't be standing there so calmly if he'd been bitten.

"He likes me. He wouldn't bite me," the little boy answered, confirming her assumption.

Still, Bailey was relieved to hear it. "And you used your uncle Gib's *toothbrush* to wash him?" she asked then.

"He needed a bath. But it's okay. I put it back."

"Somehow I don't think your uncle Gib will think it's okay when he finds out."

"You're not scared?" Kyle asked with disbelief that squinted his eyes at her.

The only thing she was afraid of was having to tell Gib that he was going to need a new toothbrush and why.

"Go get the toothbrush you used and throw it away. Then wash your hands. With warm water and lots of soap."

The small boy just stared at her as she took the mouse outside. He was still standing there when she got back. "Scoot! First the toothbrush, then the hands."

Once she was sure Kyle was on his way Bailey went to the sink to wash hers, all the while thinking that what really frightened her was cooking dinner. Mice were old hat. She'd held plenty of them in research labs. But dinner for five? That scared the pants off her.

Still and all, she gamely gathered the ingredients Jean had listed, two saucepans and turned one of the stove burners on high heat.

So far so good.

She combined everything carefully, slowly, tasting along the way until the spaghetti sauce seemed pretty fair. Nothing gourmet, but fair.

Then she set the pan on the burner and headed for the pantry for a vegetable, the bread and a package of spaghetti.

She filled the second pot with water, dumped in the whole box of noodles, and put that on another burner on high heat. While she tried to figure out how she was supposed to put cheese, garlic and tomato slices on the bread and then stand them up in the toaster without losing it all, she set the table.

That was when Gib arrived home, coming in the back door again.

Bailey wondered how long it would take her to get so accustomed to the sight of him that one look didn't give her heart palpitations. Today he wore khaki slacks and a pale cream-colored dress shirt that made his skin look all the more golden brown. Even the way he bowed his head slightly to slide off his sunglasses did something twittery to her stomach.

"Hi," she said, pleased when it elicited a smile that put those sexy lines at the corners of his eyes.

"Hi," he answered, his gaze doing a subtle fall from her hair to her face to the pink polo shirt she wore over matching shorts and on to linger at her legs for only a split second. "What's cooking?"

"Spaghetti," she said, pleased with herself for having a ready answer and dinner in the works.

"Where are Kate and Kyle?"

It was the first Bailey realized the little girl was no longer kneeling on the kitchen floor coloring with Evie. "Kate was here a minute ago. Maybe she went to make sure Kyle is washing his hands," she suggested as a way of getting around to warning Gib not to use his toothbrush if he found it still in his bathroom.

He took the whole story in stride as he set what looked to be a rolled blueprint on the counter. "Thanks for letting me know. The last time Kyle used my toothbrush to clean the mud off his shoes, put it back and I was too groggy the next morning to notice until I stuck it in my mouth. How's that for a rude awakening?"

"Yuk," she said with a laugh, thinking how nice this was, having him come home, looking relaxed and glad to be there, exchanging small talk. It was so much better than yesterday's homecoming.

"I thought we ought to do some grocery shopping after we eat tonight, anyway. I'll get a new toothbrush at the store."

Evie went over to him to hand him a crayon. He picked her up and made a face. "Looks like we need a diaper change. I'll take her upstairs and do that."

"Thanks," Bailey said, sneaking a peek over her shoulder to watch him go. She hated herself for it, but she was curious about how he looked from behind in those slacks.

Good. He looked good. But she liked the jeans better. They were tighter and showed off his taut rear end. The slacks were looser fitting and didn't have the same effect.

"There's time before we eat if you want to change clothes," she called after him.

"That's okay. I think I'll just stay the way I am."

Too bad.

She heard him say hello to Kate and Kyle as he went through the living room, but even if he hadn't she'd have known they were in there a moment later when they started to argue over what they were watching on television. Apparently Kate had changed the channel from what Kyle had originally turned on.

"You big dummy" was Kate's response to Kyle calling her a stupidhead.

Then something crashed and there was the sound of glass breaking, followed by a wail from Kate to let Bailey know she had to go into the living room to intervene.

"Kyle pusheded me!"

"I was watching my show and she changed it!"

And the lamp had fallen into a glass candy dish on the end table and broken the candy dish into bits.

Bailey made sure Kate was all right, then sent Kyle to bring her the trash can from under the sink so she could clean up the glass before anyone got hurt.

Kate was still crying just for effect, but in an ear-splitting shriek over which Bailey barely heard Kyle's shout from the kitchen.

"Just bring the trash, Kyle, and tell me when you get here. I can't hear what you're saying," Bailey called back.

He shouted again, and even though she still couldn't make out the words, there was something about the tone that told her she'd better see what he wanted. "Don't go near the glass, Kate," she warned as she got up from her knees.

It wasn't until she neared the doorway between the dining room and the kitchen that she realized Kyle was shouting, "Fire!"

Flames shot up from the burner on the stove where spaghetti sauce rolled like hot lava over the edges of the pan to feed the blaze.

"Oh my God," Bailey said, not sure what to do.

Water seemed like the answer, even though the pot with the spaghetti in it was overflowing and adding starchy white suds that only made things worse. She ran to the sink, anyway, filled a glass and threw the contents at the fire. But the flames only hissed and spat and licked even higher.

She went for more water, and while she did Kyle ran for the basement, bringing back a small fire extinguisher. Before Bailey knew what he was doing, he'd sprayed foam over the entire stove, the counters and part of the floor in front of the oven, putting the fire out.

"What happened?" Gib said from the doorway as he brought Evie in, set her on the floor and charged to the stove to turn off the burners.

But before Bailey could answer him, Evie toddled behind him into the foam, slipped and fell backward, hitting her head so hard on the tile floor that it made a sick thud and turned everyone's attention to her.

Gib was closest to the baby and reached for her.

"Don't move her!" Bailey ordered unceremoniously, rushing to Evie who was too dazed to even cry.

Bailey knelt beside the tiny tot. "It's okay, honey," she said in a soothing voice as she held the child immobile, searched her nose and ears, raised her arms one at a time, bent her legs at the knees, scanned her face, checked her pupils and lastly took her pulse.

By then Evie was crying loud and hard and fighting to get up. But not until Bailey was satisfied with her exam did she scoop the child into her lap to comfort her.

That was also when she glanced up to find Gib staring at her with raised eyebrows and an expression that let her know her actions had surprised him. More than surprised him. Stunned him.

"First aid," she said in a hurry, afraid she'd given herself away. "I took a course."

Still he looked as if he wasn't quite sure what he'd just witnessed. "You must have been the star pupil."

Dinner ended up being hamburgers at a fast-food restaurant after Bailey and Gib had done some surface cleaning of her cooking disaster, disposed of the broken glass in the living room and loaded the kids into Gib's station wagon.

Then they went to the grocery store, where Bailey's lack of knowledge about food and staple shopping was evident. Still, she managed to stock up on prepared foods and items that said Just Add Meat on the label, hoping they were easy to make and she might be able to figure out how to do it without setting fire to the kitchen.

Back at the house, Bailey and Gib put away the perishables, left the rest of the groceries in the sacks and agreed to make quick work of the kids' baths to get them to bed before they'd meet in the kitchen to finish up.

Because it was so far past their bedtime and they were tired and cranky, Gib decided to skip reading to them and told Bailey to just put the girls straight to bed after their baths—what he intended to do with Kyle.

Bailey's second round of solo baths went better than the first. She managed not to flood the floor and to only get her own clothes damp in spots. But she wasn't too sure about putting Kate and Evie to bed.

Not that she thought it was too difficult. She'd watched Gib do it her first night here and she knew it wasn't complicated. What she didn't know was how the girls would take to her doing it rather than their uncle Gib.

There was no denying that these kids loved him dearly. From the minute he came home at night, they vied for his attention, crawled all over him, and Kate and Evie jockeyed for his lap until at some point he usually ended up with one of them on each knee.

Lucky little girls was what flashed through Bailey's mind when it happened. But as she finished getting them into their pajamas, she wondered how they were going to accept her as Gib's replacement for tucking them in.

Evie didn't prove to be a problem. The baby was so weary that Bailey had only to lay her in her crib, hand her her bottle and Evie rolled onto her side and closed her eyes.

The sight of that sweet, cherubic face did a sudden, unexpected tug on Bailey's heartstrings. She couldn't resist reaching over the side to smooth Evie's downy hair, lingering just a moment to look at the baby who seemed only to have a bump on the back of her head as a result of the fall.

"I want my story," Kate announced then, pulling Bailey's attention to her.

Kate had insisted on putting on her own pajamas and hadn't done too bad a job. She'd ended with an extra button on bottom and an extra hole on top, but Bailey thought better of discouraging her by letting her know she hadn't done it perfectly.

"Remember what your uncle Gib said? It's too late tonight. He'll read you two tomorrow night."

"I want one, anyway. Tell 'im."

Telling him wouldn't make any difference. Bailey knew Gib had already finished with Kyle and gone downstairs because she'd heard him pass by the door, and if she called him to read to Kate he'd come up and firmly tell his niece no, because once he put his foot down with the kids he didn't waver.

She also knew he expected her back in the kitchen as quickly as possible to finish with the groceries. But she suddenly discovered in herself a tiny longing to have what he had with the kids and that tiny longing made *her* want to sit against Kate's headboard the way he did, wrap an arm around the small shoulder and do the bedtime story. Just this once.

"Maybe a really short book," she said to Kate, as if the two of them were thieves in the night, wondering if Kate would accept her. Hoping she would.

"From you? Not Uncle Gib?"

"Uncle Gib said no. You'll have to just slip in a short one with me or none at all. Sorry."

Kate frowned so deeply that it creased her brow, squinted her eyes and pinched her mouth. And Bailey's hopes sank.

Then the little girl said, "Okay. I like the Eloise book."

It was as if Kate had given her an early Christmas gift and Bailey's pleasure in it surprised her. But she didn't waste any time getting into position so Kate could bring the book and curl up beside her.

This was what she wanted, she reminded herself, as Kate leaned against Bailey's side. This was what made all the work she was doing, all the mishaps she was encountering, worth it. To learn what she needed to know so she could have a little girl—or a little boy—of her own and enjoy the warmth of moments like this.

Kate was asleep before the end of the book, but Bailey finished it, anyway, to give herself another moment of snuggling with the child.

Then she slipped off the bed, covered Kate with the sheet and tiptoed out of the room.

She didn't bring with her too many regrets at the ending of that encounter, though. Because now came the part of the evening Bailey looked forward to most—although she only realized it as she descended the stairs to return to the kitchen and her heart did a skip at the thought that now was the time she got to be alone with Gib. And suddenly putting canned goods in the pantry seemed more exciting than riding the rapids in an inner tube.

Gib was already busy when she got to the kitchen, and he didn't seem to hear her approach because he didn't glance her way or even break stride in taking groceries out of the sacks and setting them on the table.

Bailey couldn't help pausing in the doorway to let her eyes feast on him. He still wore the khaki slacks and the cream-colored shirt he'd had on all day, but gone was the dark stubble of his beard that he hadn't shaved before they'd left.

Why had he bothered to do it now? she wondered, almost regretting the loss of the shadow that had accentuated the stark planes of his face and given him an even more rugged handsomeness, a just barely unkempt appearance that was very masculine, very attractive.

As usual his sleeves were rolled to just below his elbows, exposing thick wrists and forearms that, for some reason Bailey couldn't explain, seemed wildly intriguing to her. Maybe because they looked so strong, so powerful.

And his hands—oh, his hands—strong and powerful-looking, too, with long, thick fingers and just a smattering of hair on the backs. They were definitely a man's hands. A hard-working man's hands. Yet she also knew them for the gentleness she'd seen innumerable times in the way he touched the kids. A gentleness that she longed to experience herself....

She pushed her thoughts away from that in a hurry and forced her feet to take her the rest of the way into the kitchen before those thoughts got any more out of line.

"Kyle asleep?" she asked in greeting as she joined Gib at the table to gather what she could carry of the groceries and to hide what had been going on in her head.

"Protesting that he wasn't tired right up to the minute his eyes closed. How about the girls?"

"Sleeping like angels," she answered, taking all she could to the pantry, passing the remnants of the fire on the stove. "I'm sorry about this," she said with a nod in that direction. "And about Evie falling because of it."

Gib joined her in the lee of the pantry door, standing close enough to unload his own arms. Close enough for her to smell the after-shave he must have used just before coming downstairs again. Close enough to feel the heat of his big body and have it raise her own temperature.

"As far as the fire goes," he said, "I did that myself once—that's why we have the extinguisher. I didn't have one before, and by the time I got the fire out I'd ruined the stove. Had to buy a new one, and while I was at it I got the fire extinguisher and gave Kyle lessons in what to do."

"I wondered why he was so prepared."

"But don't beat yourself up over it happening. I know how easy it is for the kids to distract you, something to boil over and there you are—with a fire in the kitchen."

His understanding was a relief to her as they both went back to the table for more things.

"As for Evie's fall," he continued, "*I* set her down, so if that's anyone's fault it's mine."

They were back in the pantry together, and he stopped putting cans on the shelves to look directly at her. "Besides, I got to witness proof that I don't have to worry about you taking care of the kids if one of them gets hurt. You really knew what you were doing."

"Simple first aid," she repeated her earlier explanation.

"I didn't realize first-aid classes taught anything so in depth. I thought it was just basics."

"That's all I really did. Basics." She didn't want to talk about it and find herself needing to lie to him more than she already had. She also didn't think it was a good idea to stay basking in his green-flecked gaze when it made her insides skitter around like giddy girls. So she left his gaze and the pantry.

He seemed to know he'd made her uncomfortable and let her off the hook. "Before the fire, when I got home, there didn't seem to be any more problems left over from today, though."

Or any less. But she didn't say that. "I managed to keep up a little better," she said instead, thinking there was no harm in putting as positive a spin on her day as she could. "Letting the kids play in the backyard helped."

She timed her last trip to the pantry so she'd make it when Gib was headed for the table to avoid such close proximity to him. But even as she was congratulating herself for resisting his allure, she also realized the groceries were all put away, it was late, and he might well end the evening. And deep disappointment struck, too.

He folded the bags and stashed them in the cupboard under the sink, glancing in the direction of the stove. "I know we should put some elbow grease into that, but ever since you mentioned the backyard it's been calling to me. This place is stuffy from being closed up tonight while we were gone, and nothing sounds better right now than taking a beer out there. How about it? Will you have one and join me?"

That took her off guard because she hadn't expected it, and even as she told herself she should reject the invitation and try to maintain a purely working relationship with him, she heard herself say, "That sounds great. I haven't had a beer since—" She almost said since her residency, when it had been a cheap way to celebrate the end of a long shift. But she caught herself and said, "I haven't had a beer in ages."

"Great. Then let's forget everything in here for tonight and do it."

He was probably just being courteous, she told herself, as he supplied two bottles of imported beer that had not been the cheap kind residents drank. What else was he going to do? she asked herself. He couldn't have sent her up to her room, while he got himself one and went out back to enjoy it. That would have been rude. And Gib Harden was not a rude man. So this was no more than simple courtesy and good manners. That was the only reason he'd asked her to join him. There wasn't anything more to it.

Except those giddy girls were dancing around her insides like crazy again.

She tried to tame them, took the beer he handed her and went to the back screen door he held open for her.

The porch was only a five-foot square of cement with steps leading down to the lawn. It wasn't big enough for any furniture, and rather than going out to the picnic table in the yard, Gib sat on the top step, leaving a space for Bailey beside him.

Common sense told her they'd be better off on opposite sides of the picnic table. But the giddy girls were thrilled at the prospect of sitting on that cement slab only a few inches away from Gib. And that was what she did.

He took a deep breath of night air that expanded his already big chest and raised his broad shoulders before he exhaled and said, "Feels good out here, doesn't it?"

It wasn't the summer evening that was making her feel good. But she said, "It's nice," and followed his lead to take a drink of her beer.

Even as she did, she was much too aware of everything about him. Of the curve of his hand around the beer bottle, of the way he lifted it to his mouth, of the way his lips met it, curved to it. Of the way the moonlight dusted his hair and cast a milky glow onto his profile. Of how much she liked it all....

"You're good with the kids," she blurted out in an effort to distract herself. "Did you grow up with a lot of brothers and sisters?"

He let the bottle dangle by its neck between the spread of his solid thighs. "Just Josh and me. Josh was the kids' father."

"Only the two of you. You must have been close."

"We were. Couldn't have been any closer."

"It must have made losing him all the harder," she guessed.

"Miserable. If I hadn't had Jack around, I think I would've gone off the deep end."

"Jack? The cousin who was upstairs with the kids on Saturday during our interview?"

He took another drink. "Right. Also the cop who arranged your fingerprinting. We were the Three Musketeers—Josh, Jack and me. When Josh was killed, Jack and I hung on to each other like lifelines, I guess you could say."

Where had his wife fitted into that picture? Bailey wondered. Why hadn't she been his lifeline?

But she didn't feel free to ask and sipped her own beer to refrain from it. Then she said, "Do the kids remind you of your brother?"

Gib's handsome face broke into a grin. "Kyle is the spitting image of his father. Looks like him. Acts like him. Sometimes, when I'm really missing Josh, it helps. Other times... well, other times it's a reminder and it almost hurts."

"And the girls?"

His grin softened to a smile. "They're like their momma. Melissa was a beauty. And just a little bossy—like Kate," he added, but with a great affection.

"You were fond of your sister-in-law, too."

"I'd have married her if Josh hadn't beaten me to it."

"Are we talking about a serious sibling rivalry over a woman?" Bailey teased.

"For a while. I brought Melissa home from college with me. She set eyes on Josh and liked him better."

"I don't suppose you appreciated that."

"It made me mad as hell," he said with a laugh. "We had a knock-down, drag-out fight. I still have the scar where I broke open my hand on his front tooth." He doubled up his right fist and showed it to her.

Bailey could barely make out the silvery scar across his knuckles, and even that set off the silliest idea that she wanted to press her lips to that same spot. To run her tongue across the big bones of his hand...

"Sounds bad," she said in a voice that was too breathless and throaty for her liking.

"It was." But he was still smiling at the memory. "We beat each other to a pulp. Didn't stop even when Jack turned the hose on us. Kept at it until we were both exhausted and bloody and battered. Couldn't see through the black eyes. Teeth broken. Faces and a lot more bruised. Noses bleeding. We were a pretty pair, I can tell you. Good thing we were evenly matched, or one of us might have killed the other."

"Then what happened?"

"Jack took us to the emergency room to get patched up."

Bailey laughed. "No, I mean to your relationship with your brother, with Melissa."

He laughed, too, at his own misunderstanding and taking her question too literally. And Bailey liked the sound much too much. It was deep and warm and sensual and seemed to wrap around her like an angora sweater.

"Josh and I didn't speak for a while. So neither did Melissa and I, because by then she was all his. But when I cooled off, Jack made peace between us."

Bailey couldn't imagine the other woman picking anyone over Gib. But that was not a thought she should have been having.

"And after that everything was all right?" she asked, to keep herself on track.

"Pretty much. Jack introduced me to Angie—the woman I ended up with." He cocked his head at a rakish angle and looked at her from the corner of his eye. "But that's a whole other story you don't want to hear."

His tone said he didn't want to tell it, and he drank from his beer to put a seal to it.

Bailey tasted her own again and then said, "Did you still have feelings for Melissa even after she married your brother?"

He shook his head. "Feelings go away. Even strong ones." He seemed suddenly slightly more serious and turned enough to look straight at her, his expression wry. "At least that's what I keep telling myself—feelings go away if you just ignore them."

What kind of feelings? Feelings like her attraction to him? Feelings like those giddy girls who danced in her insides every time he got near her?

Feelings Gib was having for her?

Couldn't be...

Except that as he held her eyes with his, she somehow knew she wasn't alone in this attraction that was swirling around them. That he was having some kind of feelings for her, just as she was having them for him.

Feelings that kept his eyes searching her face. That raised his hand in slow motion to lay his palm against her cheek, to ease her toward him at the same moment he eased toward her.

And then he did what she'd been trying not to wish he would do. He kissed her. A kiss just like him—warm, gentle, sexy. A kiss that calmed the giddy girls inside her, that heated them up and left them lazy, languorous and wanting more.

But they weren't going to get it.

Because as quickly as it began, Gib ended the kiss, drew away from her, hands and lips and even body, as he set his elbows to his knees, bent over them and shook his head.

"I shouldn't have done that," he said.

And even though Bailey agreed, she couldn't say it out loud, because knowing he shouldn't have kissed her didn't take away how wonderful the kiss had been. Or make her regret it.

"Maybe I'd better say good-night," she said instead.

He nodded as if he thought it was the right thing to do, too. But the frown that pulled at his brows looked as if he wasn't so sure he wanted her to go in spite of that.

"I'll see you tomorrow," she said, as she stood with her beer bottle.

"Tomorrow," he answered, and she honestly didn't know if that single word had held promise in his tone or if it was just wishful thinking on her part.

But she couldn't stay to explore it, as common sense finally kicked in and reminded her he was her boss. He was a man she was deceiving. And being there with him was only a temporary arrangement with purposes that didn't include getting involved with him.

Bailey didn't say any more. She opened the screen door and went in.

Only once she was safely on the other side, she couldn't resist looking back at Gib, at his wide shoulders, his straight spine, the curve of his hairline against his neck. And more than anything she wanted to be out there with him again.

But she fought it, spinning away from the appealing sight he made to push herself through the house, up the stairs and into her room like a runner headed for the finish line.

And once inside she locked her door.

Not against Gib getting in.

But as a symbolic gesture to keep her from going back out to him.

Chapter Six

When Bailey's alarm went off at two o'clock the next morning, she was deeply, soundly asleep. For a moment she didn't know where she was or why music was playing into the darkness of the middle of the night.

Then she remembered.

She'd decided that if she couldn't get anything accomplished on the housecleaning front during the day because she was too busy trying to keep up with the kids, she'd get a jump on it by cutting into her sleep. Maybe in the quiet of predawn hours she could actually learn to do the chores she'd been hired for and in the process also gain some control over the place. Functioning on only a little sleep wasn't anything new to her, after all. She'd done it plenty as an intern, as a resident. She did it whenever she had late-night babies to deliver now. She could do it for this.

Then, when she got good at keeping house and juggling the kids during the day, she could go back to sleeping through the night.

The trouble was, as she lay in her bed, her body cried out to let it stay there.

Until the image of Gib popped into her mind.

She pictured him impressed with her mastery of the job, thrilled with his clean, organized house. It was a satisfying fantasy.

But the truth was, the idea of seeing him before he left for work was what really got her up.

She wanted to shower and wash her hair, to be perfectly turned out so that when he came downstairs he'd find her looking her best, but she resisted the urge. Running the water in her bathroom was likely to wake Gib. Besides, she'd gotten used to fixing herself up during the kids' nap and liked being fresh for his homecoming and their evening together.

She did use a few minutes to dress in a silk sweatsuit, apply just enough makeup to be presentable and run a comb through her hair, though, so she still looked put together before she ever left her bedroom to go downstairs as quietly as she possibly could.

The first order of business was the cooking-fire disaster. A huge yawn grabbed hold of her as she switched on the kitchen light. She fought a wave of weariness that washed over her and urged her back to bed. It would pass, she told herself. It always did at the hospital. So instead of heeding the call to rest, she set her sights on the stove.

But somehow the monotony of scrubbing the appliance and floor all by herself in the silence of the house didn't revive her the way a medical emergency or delivering a baby in a brightly lit hospital with a lot of other people around did. And an hour later, even though she'd actually done a fair job of cleaning the fire, food and foam mess, the weariness hadn't passed. In fact, it was worse, and she was having trouble keeping her eyes open.

A catnap was what she needed. Interns, residents and obstetricians learned to use them to great advantage, and so Bailey decided just a short one on the couch would do her wonders. Then she'd tackle straightening the cupboards, cleaning the dining and living rooms and have this place whipped into shape by the time Gib came downstairs.

And so, with visions of his surprised, pleased, handsome face in her head, she lay on the couch to catch forty winks.

"...And winking Mary-buds begin to ope their golden eyes: With everything that pretty is, My lady sweet, arise..."

The deep, seductive voice drifted into Bailey's mind on soft wings and made her smile even as she fought its tug to wake her up. *What a nice change,* she thought, *a disk jockey who recites poetry.* And she waited for more.

Instead she heard, "How about opening just one eye and telling me you aren't sleeping down here because something's wrong? Then I'll leave you alone if you want me to."

Those quiet words brought Bailey slightly more awake to wonder what the guy on the radio alarm was talking about.

But it wasn't a guy on the radio, she realized suddenly. It was Gib's voice she was hearing. Gib's masculine, earthy, subtly sexy voice.

Why was he in her bedroom?

Curiosity and a little rush of excitement at the possibilities finally brought her awake enough to open her eyes just a crack.

He was sitting a few inches away. On the coffee table.

The coffee table.

She wasn't in bed. She was on the couch. In his living room. And the sun was just a hint around the edges of the drapes covering the picture window.

Forty winks had turned into a lot more.

She closed her eyes again, as if daggers had been shot into them, and groaned.

"Are you sick, sweetie?" he asked sympathetically, bending near enough so that the warmth of his breath caressed her cheek. Or maybe it was the endearment that felt so good.

"No, I'm not sick," she answered, opening her eyes again to find him leaning forward, elbows to thighs spread wide, big hands dangling between them with a cup of steaming coffee in each one.

"The bed upstairs have lumps in it?" he asked.

"No, the bed's fine." She pushed herself to a sitting position and accepted the cup of coffee he held out to her. "Thanks."

"You walk in your sleep and you ended up down here?" Another guess.

She sipped the coffee gratefully and shook her head. "I set my alarm to come down and get some work done—"

"I wondered what elves had been in the kitchen."

"When I finished with the stove I thought I'd take just a tiny nap before I moved on to anything else and—"

"Ah, so that's all there is to it. I thought there might be more," he said, with a tilt of just one corner of his mouth.

"More? You mean more cleaning? I wish there had been. That was the plan. But here I am wasting hours of time I could have used," she said with a glance at the country oak clock on the wall in the corner. It was nearly six.

He chuckled slightly. "No, no more cleaning," he said with a hint of mischievousness in his voice and in his expression.

He took a drink of his own coffee and came up from it with that quirky smile still in place. "I thought you might have wanted to see me off to work. Maybe share a little breakfast. Or slap me across the face?"

Bailey finally caught on to the fact that he was teasing her. "Slap you across the face?" she repeated, playing along.

He only raised one eyebrow in answer to that.

The kiss the night before was what he was referring to, though he didn't look or sound contrite about it, the way he had then.

"Or worse yet," he added, "I was worried you might be waiting down here to quit."

Again, because of the kiss—that was the unspoken subject they were discussing.

That kiss had done a lot of things to her—thrilled her, enticed her, heated her blood, left her wanting more—but it hadn't made her consider quitting this job. If anything, a secret part of her couldn't help wishing he'd do it again. Right there and then.

"I only came down to clean," she said, to avoid her own thoughts.

He looked so good freshly shaven, his hair combed, his hazel eyes bright, that she could hardly regret the early hour and the effort when it got her time with him and a chance to see him like that.

"I don't want you doing this to yourself."

She didn't think he meant torturing herself with the kind of thoughts she was having about him. "Do what to myself?"

"Missing sleep, getting up in the middle of the night to clean. That'll wear you out quicker than the kids will."

"It's okay. I've functioned on only a little sleep a lot of times."

"How come?"

She'd walked right into the breach. "Oh, you know. Studying all night, things like that."

"Well, you don't need to be doing it around here. It's bad enough the kids run you ragged during the day. If you don't sleep at night, you won't last long."

Guilt stabbed her at the secret knowledge that she wasn't going to be here more than a few months, anyway. But she felt something else, too. Regret at that fact?

She pushed it aside. "I did a pretty good job on the stove, though."

"Mmm. Just be sure to clean out the pans under the burners or turning them on again is liable to start a fire all over."

Okay, so she'd done a pretty good job for someone who didn't notice pans under the burners.

"On the other hand," he said with a glint in his eyes that made the green flecks stand out. "If getting up to clean in the middle of the night means I find you on the couch when I come down here, maybe I should reconsider. It's a nice way to start my day."

A slow, honeyed warmth rolled through her with that. Helped along by his steady gaze, it somehow had the power to elicit a physical response.

"Waking up to poetry isn't too bad, either. What was it?"

"Shakespeare."

"Ah." She nodded. "My education was heavy in math and science, light in arts and literature, I'm afraid." And wasn't it interesting that this rugged construction worker could recite it? Interesting and unexpected and charming. But then the more she got to know about him, the more interesting and unique and charming she found him. "You're much better than an alarm clock."

He laughed. "Thanks. I think."

She sipped from her cup again and then held it up as if in toast to him. "You make good coffee, too. Is there anything you don't do well? No, wait, I know— you're not good at choosing housekeepers."

He grinned at her. "I'm not so bad at that, either."

This really was nice, Bailey thought. The early hour seemed to have lent them both a more relaxed attitude, thrown in a touch of comraderie and more than a touch of intimacy to go with it. The banter, the flirting—she was enjoying it all. Enjoying Gib. And it occurred to her that she wouldn't mind sleeping on the couch every night, if every morning brought times like this with him.

A dangerous thought.

A more dangerous feeling.

"Can I make you toast or something for breakfast?' she asked then, to put this back on a safer course.

But before he could answer, a safer course arrived in the form of Kate coming downstairs to silently curl up in one corner of the couch with her security blanket, her stuffed monkey and her thumb.

Gib sat up a little straighter, putting a small but telling distance between them at the first sight of his niece. "I've been getting into work early all week to do some catch-up myself," he said as he stood. "I think I'll just grab a doughnut between here and there. Thanks, anyway." Then he pointed a long index finger at her. "But no more nocturnal cleaning. We'll get on top of it together. Maybe I'll have my folks take the kids for the weekend and we'll do it then."

Bailey nodded her agreement, not because she was averse to cutting her sleep short, but because the attraction between the two of them was too strong and getting stronger every minute. She knew the less time they spent in cozy morning chats when her defenses were low, the better.

Then he said, "We need to do some clothes and shoe shopping for the kids. Think you can load them into the station wagon and meet me at the mall at four this afternoon? We can have some dinner at the food court and that way maybe it won't end up being a late night for them."

And there wouldn't be any chance of her setting fire to the kitchen. "Sure, I think I can handle the station wagon and find my way to the mall."

"Great. There's a children's store at the north end. Just wait for me there. The car keys are on the counter."

"Okay."

"Well," he said then. He was up and ready to walk out but seemed to stall. Instead his eyes stayed on her a moment before he tore them away. "I'll head out the back now. Have a good day."

"You too."

He nodded, hesitated, but in the end kissed Kate and took his coffee cup to the kitchen.

And even though Bailey wouldn't have minded one of those kisses for herself, he still left her with the lingering glow of that warmth he'd wrapped the start of her day in.

Which put her back on that dangerous course fraught with dangerous feelings.

She was just too contented to care.

"Evie gots the potty pan on her head."

Kate's announcement brought Bailey from changing the crib sheets into the girls' bathroom where Evie did, indeed, have the potty chair's removable catch basin upturned on her head. Luckily it was empty— the only positive side to the fact that Bailey was not having much success in her first attempt at training the youngest Harden. So much for the technique in the baby book she'd brought with her.

"See?" Evie said, preening and showing off her headgear.

Gib had told Bailey to wait on the toilet training, but she'd been hoping to surprise him. She gave up that idea when, standing there modeling her makeshift hat, Evie proceeded to wet on the floor. For the third time that morning.

"On the potty, Evie. You're supposed to do that on the potty like a big girl. Like Kate," she groaned.

The toddler just smiled serenely.

Bailey cleaned her up, diapered her, then mopped the bathroom floor.

She'd opted for a change of scenery today, mounted an all-out assault on the kids' bedrooms and baths and had actually made some headway with Kate and Evie's room. The bathroom floor hadn't been where she had planned to start, but since it was already mopped, she moved on to the rest of that room while the girls took out toys she'd just put away and Kyle acted very strangely.

He was spying on Bailey from outside the door to the hallway.

She thought he was playing a game, although it had lasted longer than anything she'd ever seen any of the kids do, and he was very serious and intent on it. And it didn't seem like much fun.

"Wouldn't you like to play with one of your games or something, Kyle?" Bailey called to him when she saw him sneak a peek at her, then dodge behind the jamb when he realized she'd seen him.

"No. That's okay," he called back without showing his face.

Very strange.

But he wasn't hurting anything, he wasn't into mischief, he wasn't even making a mess, so she figured whatever he was pretending must have been less boring in his mind than it seemed in reality, and she went on about her business.

Bathrooms, she discovered, were not pretty things to clean. Especially not bathrooms that hadn't been cleaned in a while.

On the other hand, she seemed to be able to do it without causing catastrophes, so that was something.

It was disheartening to find the girls' bedroom torn apart and littered with toys again and the bed messed up from Kate jumping on it when she finished, but she was almost getting used to nothing ever staying the way she left it. At least the bathroom was clean. For now.

She told the girls she was going into Kyle's room, and since they were busy playing, she left them there.

Kyle, though, followed close at her heels.

While she straightened his room and changed his sheets, his spying turned less clandestine. He stood next to his dresser drawers and watched her openly.

It didn't make sense, but Bailey was hardly experienced in the way of kids, and when she couldn't engage him in conversation or persuade him to do anything else, she opted for ignoring him.

Only when she headed for his bathroom did he spring into action. He literally jumped between her and his closed bathroom door, blocking her from going through it.

"Mine is okay," he said, sounding desperate, his eyes open wide.

After finding a peanut-butter sandwich behind the commode, doll heads stuck on the ends of the towel bar, a smelly tennis shoe in the back of the vanity and various other accumulated detritus in the girls' bathroom, Bailey could only image what was in Kyle's that he didn't want her to see.

"I need to clean in there. It doesn't matter how messy it is."

His eyes got bigger. "You can't. It's not dirty."

"Move, Kyle. I need to get in there."

"You can't."

"I have to." Bailey put a hand on his small shoulder and eased him out of the way.

Expecting to see the toilet overflowed or something equally awful, she was pleasantly surprised. The bathroom wasn't any better than Kate and Evie's had been, but it wasn't any worse, either. And nothing in it looked like something for Kyle to be concerned about.

Then Bailey remembered her first night here and his modesty about his bath.

She turned to find him standing in the doorway.

"Why don't you go play while I clean? If you don't see me do it, it won't even be like I was ever in here," she suggested.

He just stared at her very solemnly and shook his head. He looked as if he was facing a firing squad—bravely, stoically, resigned to his fate.

There was nothing Bailey could do but go back to ignoring him.

Since the toilet was her least favorite of the cleaning chores, that was what she turned to. When she did, Kyle lunged a second time to block her, pressing his back against the side of the tank.

"Kyle—"

"Nobody uses this toilet," he said, as if it were outlawed.

"I'm not going to use it. I'm just going to clean it. Don't you like anyone but you using your bathroom?"

"You can't clean it, neither."

The seat and the lid were down. "Did you flush something you shouldn't have and plug it up?" she asked.

His face paled. "You can't flush it. Not never."

"It's okay if you did. You won't be in trouble."

"You can't flush it!"

Bailey lifted the seat. There was nothing in the bowl other than clear water with a ring around its top edge, as if it hadn't been cleaned or flushed in some time.

She reached for the handle to flush it now and see what the problem was.

"No!"

"It's okay."

"You can't!"

"Why can't I?"

"Just 'cuz."

"Is it clogged?"

"No. Just 'cuz."

"This is silly." Again she reached for the handle.

"No! No! You'll kill him!"

"Who will I kill?"

"Howard. He's 'fraid you'll kill Howard," Kate said from the doorway. Apparently she and Evie had come to see what the commotion was. "It's Howard's 'quar'um.'"

"You weren't spose to tell!" Kyle shouted at his sister, rushing her, shoving her out of the way and running past.

"Who's Howard?" Bailey asked, not having any idea what a quarum was, either, but thinking to start with the easiest question.

Kate merely stretched out her arm and pointed toward the toilet tank.

Bailey lowered the seat and lid, then lifted the tank's cover.

Quarum was aquarium. And Howard was a frog. Sitting atop a piece of wood balanced on the flushing apparatus.

Bailey was impressed by the small boy's ingenuity. The frog essentially had everything a frog needed— land, sea and food, too, if the flies floating on the water were any indication.

Like mice, frogs were familiar to Bailey, and she reached into the tank to lift Howard out, taking him with her to find Kyle.

But finding Kyle was harder than solving the mystery of the toilet, and it wasn't until Kate prompted her that she discovered him in his closet, perched on a basketball in the deepest corner of it, rocking back and forth nervously.

Standing in the closet's doorway, Bailey held up the frog. "Howard, I presume?"

Kyle just looked at her with terrified eyes.

"It's okay. I'm not afraid of frogs, either."

Still his lower lip quivered.

"Are you worried I'll let him go the way I did the mouse yesterday?" she asked, thinking he'd probably had Howard longer and was more attached.

But Kyle just shook his head. "You'll tell Uncle Gib I been keepin' him and he'll go 'way an' never not come back like my mom and dad and Angie."

Bailey stopped short at that, realizing that for some reason she'd touched a nerve with the little boy. "Your uncle Gib would never go away just because you've been hiding a frog in the toilet tank, Kyle. He'd never go away at all."

"Uh-huh, he would. Everybody else does. If I'm bad."

Her heart went out to him. Such small shoulders to be carrying such a burden—imagined or not. And she suddenly felt more inept at the call to ease that bur-

SILHOUETTE®

N IMPORTANT MESSAGE
ROM THE EDITORS OF
ILHOUETTE®

ear Reader,

ecause you've chosen to read one of our
ne romance novels, we'd like to say
thank you"! And, as a **special** way to
hank you, we've selected <u>four more</u> of the
ooks you love so well, **and** a Cuddly
eddy Bear to send you absolutely ***FREE!***

lease enjoy them with our compliments...

Nora Flavin

Senior Editor,
Silhouette Special Edition

*P.S. And because we value our
customers, we've attached
something extra inside ...*

EDITOR'S
**FREE
GIFT
SEAL**
THANK YOU

PEEL OFF SEAL AND
PLACE INSIDE

DETACH AND MAIL CARD TODAY!

PLACE FREE GIFT SEAL HERE

YES! I have placed my Editor's "thank you" seal in the space provided above. Please send me 4 free books and a Cuddly Teddy Bear. I understand I am under no obligation to purchase any books, as explained on the back and on the opposite page.

235 CIS A4UD (U-SIL-SE-10/96)

_____
NAME

_____
ADDRESS   APT.

_____
CITY   STATE   ZIP

Thank you!

THE SILHOUETTE READER SERVICE™: HERE'S HOW IT WORKS

Accepting free books places you under no obligation to buy anything. You may keep the books and gift and return the shipping statement marked "cancel". If you do not cancel, about a month later we will send you 6 additional novels, and bill you just $3.34 each plus 25¢ delivery and applicable sales tax, if any*. That's the complete price, and—compared to cover prices of $3.99 each—quite a bargain! You may cancel at any time, but if you choose to continue, every month we'll send you 6 more books, which you may either purchase at the discount price…or return to us and cancel your subscription.

*Terms and prices subject to change without notice. Sales tax applicable in N.Y.

If offer card is missing write to: Silhouette Reader Service, 3010 Walden Ave., P.O. Box 1867, Buffalo, NY 14240-1867

BUSINESS REPLY MAIL
FIRST-CLASS MAIL   PERMIT NO. 717   BUFFALO, NY

POSTAGE WILL BE PAID BY ADDRESSEE

SILHOUETTE READER SERVICE
3010 WALDEN AVE
PO BOX 1867
BUFFALO, NY 14240-9952

NO POSTAGE
NECESSARY
IF MAILED
IN THE
UNITED STATES

den than she had at anything else she'd faced here yet.

She squatted down to sit on the heels of her feet so she could be at eye level with him. "You're not bad, Kyle. And your mom and dad didn't go away because of anything you did. They didn't go away because they wanted to. They didn't have a choice." And she didn't know what else to say. That God or angels had taken them to heaven? Did he even recognize that they were dead? Did he even have a concept of death?

Maybe Gib's ex-wife was a safer subject to address. "And as for Angie, she didn't leave because of you—"

"She did so. I heared her. She didn't want us kids. She said nobody'd want a bunch of kids that wasn't hers."

Lord. Had the other woman actually said that? Had she felt it about these three great kids? And what could Bailey say to Kyle who'd heard it and been so hurt by it?

"And her and Uncle Gib hollered at each other," Kyle went on, "and then she went away and Uncle Gib was sad. And now he'll get mad at me and go 'way, too."

"He won't. He really won't." Bailey hated how ineffective she sounded. "Look. What if we take Howard outside and fix him a home of his own? We'll say we found him in the yard today. Your uncle Gib won't mind that. And we'll never let him know you were hiding Howard in the toilet so he won't have anything to get mad at. Would that be all right?"

Kyle thought it over. "Can you do that?" he asked dubiously.

"Believe me, I'm better with frogs than with some other things." Like knowing how to reassure this child that his uncle wouldn't leave him, or if she was doing the right thing by conspiring to keep this from Gib.

Kyle kept rocking nervously back and forth on his basketball perch a while longer, watching her, judging whether or not she knew what she was talking about, Bailey thought.

"Really. I may not be good at cooking and cleaning, but frogs are another story," she tried again.

Finally Kyle stopped rocking and stood up. "Okay."

She could tell he was still skeptical, that she hadn't convinced him, either, that she could take care of Howard or that Gib wouldn't abandon Kyle the way so many people had before, and she doubted her lecture on the biology of amphibians was an adequate compensation.

But it was all she had to work with.

Because she honestly didn't know how else to help, and at least that seemed to distract him.

So she spent the rest of the day fashioning a pond, beach and a cage for the frog rather than accomplishing any more of the work she'd been hired for. Again.

It might have been worth it, though, if only she'd felt as if she'd done some real good for her young charge.

But she didn't. Instead, by the time she put Kyle and the girls down for their naps, she felt woefully inadequate on yet another front—this one even more important than cooking or cleaning.

By the time the kids woke up later that afternoon, Bailey was ready for their shopping excursion. She had on her red blouse tucked into her best white linen slacks, and had applied light makeup and caught her hair back in a white leather headband.

Still, from the minute Evie made her first peep to let Bailey know she was awake until they needed to leave for the mall, Bailey rushed around. She marveled at how much face and hand washing, hair combing, shoe tying, diaper changing, packing and loading it took to accomplish getting the kids spruced up and loaded into Gib's station wagon. But it was a fact of life.

The mall wasn't far from the house, and she found it without difficulty. In fact, it took less time to drive there than it had to get all three kids strapped and buckled into the car. Less time than it took to unstrap and unbuckle them. Less time than it took her to figure out how to set up the stroller and secure Evie into it.

Once she had, she barely managed to get to the children's store by a quarter after four, and since Gib had said four she expected that he would be there waiting for them. He wasn't inside the front doors, so she herded the kids down the main aisle to look for him.

The place was big—huge, actually. It offered everything from kids' furniture to toys to shoes to clothing and anything imaginable in between. Moms and dads and kids milled around among the racks, stacks and shelves, but in all of the faces Bailey scanned she didn't find the one that made her pulse race just to think about.

"Your uncle Gib must not be here yet, after all," she finally concluded when they'd come back around to the front again.

But when she looked down, she discovered she was talking to herself. Or at least to herself and Evie in the stroller below her. Kyle and Kate were gone.

Bailey spun around and spotted Kyle going up steps to a big boxed-in slide in a play area a few feet away, and the initial uneasiness that had struck at that first realization that the kids weren't where they were supposed to be ebbed. She still couldn't see Kate but thought that surely the little girl was with her brother.

Only the longer she watched Kyle and searched for signs of Kate, the more she began to realize that Kate wasn't with him.

"Kate?" she called, glancing full circle around the area in which she was standing.

But Kate was nowhere around her, either.

"Kyle?" she called then to the small boy as he landed at the bottom of the slide and headed for the stairs again. "Is Kate with you?"

"Nope," he called back.

A knot formed in the pit of Bailey's stomach. Where could the little girl have gone off to? She'd been right there with her a minute ago.

Bailey called Kate's name again, pushed Evie's stroller in the general vicinity, stood on tiptoe to scan even farther, but there was no Kate.

The knot in Bailey's stomach tightened.

She told Kyle to make sure he stayed in the play area and pushed the stroller up the main aisle again, then up and down all the rest, then between the racks, all the while calling for Kate. But the little girl seemed to have disappeared into thin air.

Bailey speeded up her pace and retraced her steps, suddenly unable to stop thinking about all the kidnapping stories she'd ever heard.

What if Kate wasn't in the store anymore? What if someone had snatched her? What if she'd wandered out on her own and gotten lost? What if someone had grabbed her, pretending to help her?

Bailey's throat was so tight that it felt closed off. Beads of perspiration dotted her upper lip. She could hear her heart pounding in her ears. Her grip on the stroller's handle was white knuckled.

Where could the child have gone? Of all the kids in that place, why wasn't just one of them Kate?

Bailey was on the verge of hyperventilating and had to pause to catch her breath.

Panic wasn't going to help, she told herself, wondering at the same time at her own reaction. She'd faced life-threatening medical emergencies with more detachment than losing sight of one almost-four-year-old girl.

But reminding herself of that didn't help.

"Kate!" she shouted, hearing the rise of desperation in her own voice.

Still there was no answer, no Kate.

How could this have happened? she asked herself. How could she be so bad at this? How could she be so slow at getting the hang of everything, at foreseeing problems, at even keeping track of one small child?

"Kate! Where are you?" she called again.

Just then she spotted Gib coming toward her and wondered how she was going to tell him she'd lost one of the kids.

"I can't find Kate!" she blurted out when he was within earshot.

He must have seen how upset she was, because when he reached her he put a big, steadying hand on her shoulder and squeezed. "It's okay," he said calmly. "Come over here."

His hand slid down her arm to her elbow, and he urged her toward the front of the store, not far from where she'd been when she'd realized Kate and Kyle weren't there anymore. With both hands on her shoulders now, Gib eased her between a rack of clothing and the glass display window.

And there was Kate, standing in the midst of the mannequins that were dressed to exhibit the new fall offerings, posing along with them and drawing a crowd out in the mall.

The sight was too funny and Bailey was too relieved not to laugh. Her whole body deflated and she unwittingly relaxed back into Gib, where he stood behind her, his hands still on her shoulders.

"Scared you, did she?" he whispered in her ear.

"Terrified me," she answered through her own laughter, some of it at herself. And as the fear receded, something else took its place—a tingling at every spot where her body met Gib's.

"This is Kate's favorite thing—she wanders off to pretend she's modeling clothes in the store windows. I should have warned you. She's good at it, too. Look at how long she can stand perfectly still and blend in with the mannequins? Now wait a minute.... See, she even changes poses."

They were both laughing at the little girl's antics again, but Bailey was all too aware of the cozy intimacy of the way they were standing. Like doting parents. Like a loving couple.

It felt too wonderful to let it go on, but she had to argue with herself to finally actually remind Gib

they'd come to shop and have him let go of her to re-
trieve Kate.

But somehow even when he had, the tingling stayed
behind and turned into a glow that lasted through their
whole trip.

She liked the man entirely too much, she realized as
the evening wore on. Liked the way he looked even
with the shadow of his beard showing, even dressed in
his work clothes. Liked the sound of his deep baritone voice. Liked the way lines appeared at the corners of his eyes when he smiled. Liked the way he was
with the kids. The way he teased her. The way he
looked at her. The way he made her feel—interesting,
feminine, attractive, sexy. She just plain liked everything about him.

And she didn't know how to curb the attraction that
was growing between them, although she thought
about it as she followed him home later that evening—he and Kyle in his truck up ahead of her and the
girls in the station wagon. Worse yet, she didn't know
if she *wanted* to curb the attraction, even though she
knew she should.

Because something about being with him seemed to
complete her. And she couldn't change that, no matter how often she forced herself to remember that their
time together was only temporary and that when she
confessed what she was really doing there, who she
really was, all that was so good between them would
probably be canceled out.

For now she was with him, and it felt too right to
argue against.

So maybe, for just the little while she was working
for him, having his company and all the feelings he
inspired in her were just a fringe benefit.

And maybe, she told herself, she should relax slightly and enjoy it....

Once they got home, Gib took the kids and packages upstairs while Bailey loaded the washing machine with the bedsheets she'd stripped off earlier and the clothes that filled the hamper to overflowing. Then she went upstairs, too, and did her part of the nightly bath and bedtime routine.

As Gib read to the kids when they were finished, Bailey went back downstairs to put the laundry into the dryer and found she'd done something wrong because the laundry room floor was flooded.

"Too much detergent or too many things in the machine, or both," Gib said, startling her as she mopped up a few minutes later.

"I'm beginning to wonder if there's anything I can do right," she muttered more to herself than to him. She was still smarting from both the day's events with Kyle and losing Kate at the mall—things that weighed much more heavily on her than all of her other failures here, even if the incident with Kate had ended humorously.

"I understand you're pretty good with frogs," Gib said in consolation, crossing his arms over his chest and propping a hip on the kitchen table that was only a few feet from the laundry room's open door.

"Frogs?" she repeated, wondering if the man was a mind reader.

"It's okay. Our Miss Kate is not a good secret keeper. I just got to hear all about a certain frog named Howard who's been living in Kyle's toilet but was relocated today—thanks to you."

Bailey made a face. "Does Kyle know you know?"

"He heard Kate spill the beans. Then he hit her in the stomach. After I'd dealt with that, he chimed in to tell me how you aren't afraid of frogs or mice—big points with him—that you know all kinds of funny names for them, and that you also know—I'm quoting here—where frogses' hearts and livers and guts are, and why that thingy puffs up in frogses' throats."

But curiosity tinged his tone and Bailey thought that it was Gib alone who was wondering why she was so knowledgeable when it came to such things. In fact, she wasn't sure if she was just being paranoid or if there also might be just a hint of suspicion in his voice, too.

"Basic biology," she said.

"Basic biology. Basic first aid. A degree in chemistry you don't use... I'm never too sure what I'm going to learn about you next."

She wasn't being paranoid. He was wondering about her, all right. Time to change the subject. But not only because she didn't want to get into her own background. More important than dodging that was to let him know what had been troubling Kyle about her discovery of Howard. So she filled Gib in on the little boy's fear of being left again, on what Kyle knew Gib's ex-wife had said.

"Kyle heard that?" he asked with a deep frown.

"Seems so."

"Damn it."

She glanced up from her mopping in time to see him shaking his head angrily and staring at the floor in what looked like disgust.

Bailey remembered Gib telling her that he'd inherited the kids at a time that wasn't altogether opportune, but from what Kyle had said it seemed as if the kids had been what had really torn the marriage apart.

She was finished with the floor by then, and once she rinsed and stored the mop she joined him, leaning her back against the wall just outside the laundry room door to face him. She didn't have any right to pry, and yet the more her attraction to Gib grew, the more her curiosity got the better of her and the more compelled she was to ask questions she had no business asking.

"*Did* your wife leave because of the kids?"

He raised his gaze from the floor. "You want a sandwich? I make a great one but it always ends up huge. How about splitting it with me?"

"Okay," she said, certain that she'd ventured off limits and this was his way of letting her know.

But once he'd built a club sandwich with all the trimmings and they were at the table to eat it, he said, "The kids were just the straw that broke the back of my marriage. They didn't come into a solid, happy situation and single-handedly destroy it. We were having problems before that."

She took a bite of her half of the sandwich, told him how good it was and waited for him to go on, hoping he would without prompting.

"Angie is a corporate executive," he said when he got started again. "She works for the state's biggest insurance company. Bright, beautiful and ambitious. Her goal is to be CEO within the next seven years and I think she'll make it. But I didn't fit the profile of a CEO's husband. I don't wear a suit to work. Don't drive a prestigious car. Don't talk stocks or bonds or buyouts or golden parachutes at cocktail parties. My hands get dirty," he said, holding them up palms out.

They weren't dirty now. But they were great hands. And she liked them much, much more than the manicured variety she encountered in the men she usually ran into.

"To be blunt," Gib went on, "my wife was ashamed of me."

"That's crazy," Bailey said, before she'd even thought about the wisdom of voicing what flashed through her mind. But to her it *was* ridiculous. And so must his ex-wife be if she let this man go.

Gib gave her the one-sided smile and said, "Thanks." Then he went on, "I didn't want to think so at the time, but in retrospect I'd have to say Angie probably wouldn't have been around too much longer, anyway. The kids just speeded the process."

And remembering it seemed to cost him his appetite, because he pushed his plate away, even though he'd only eaten part of his sandwich.

Bailey had had enough food, too. But she hadn't had enough of what he was talking about. "Didn't she like kids in general, or was it just raising someone else's that she couldn't handle?"

She saw his eyebrows pull together for a split second when she referred to what Kyle had heard, and she knew it wasn't only a sore point with the little boy. It was a sore point with Gib, too.

"In better times we'd talked about having kids of our own. She only wanted one. She thought that between the two of us, one would be manageable. At some unspecified later date. That was okay—one kid was fine with me and I was in no hurry. But three? And somebody else's? She was not happy about that. Not at all."

"She hadn't agreed to take the kids when your brother and sister-in-law approached you about the will?"

"She'd agreed. She just hadn't expected it to happen any more than I had. It was a shock. But I'd always liked my nieces and nephew. And they were my blood. It was different for Angie. It probably would be for anyone."

Bailey wasn't so sure about that, but all she said was, "So the kids moved in and your wife moved out?"

"Not right away. I did everything I could so her life wouldn't be any more disrupted than it needed to be by their coming but—" he shrugged and laughed "—you know how things are around here. That was impossible. I hired help but it didn't matter. The kids were in a bad way—they'd lost their mom and dad, they'd been uprooted, they were scared, grieving, acting up. Kyle had started to wet the bed. Kate had nightmares and woke up shrieking almost every night—poor things were a mess. And Angie just wasn't up to it all."

"Like me, today with Kyle," Bailey confessed, feeling all the worse that the little boy had suffered for her ineptitude.

Gib frowned again. "What do you think you did wrong?"

"I just . . . I didn't know *what* to do. What to say. I told him you weren't going to leave him, but it didn't seem to help. The frog stuff was all I could come up with to get his mind off it."

"Did you think you could wipe away all the damage of losing his mother and father, of coming here into a less than perfect situation, and going through a divorce on top of it all, with just the right words?''

Something like that. ''I thought I should have been able to help him more than I did.''

Gib covered her hand where it lay on the table in a fist, cupping his big, strong callused palm over it and sending lightning bolts all the way up her arm in response.

''You did just fine, Bailey. You reassured him and then got him thinking about something else.''

But she'd also conspired to keep part of what had gone on from Gib, and that didn't feel like the best way to have dealt with the issue of Kyle's fear of Gib's abandoning him just because he did something wrong. ''I don't know,'' she said, all of her doubts in her voice because as much as she would have liked to believe she'd done some good, she just didn't.

''You're selling yourself short,'' Gib said into her thoughts. ''Kids are a pretty good judge of people, for the most part, and my three think highly of you. That says something about what you're doing.''

His eyes held hers, their green flecks sparkling with what looked like appreciation that she didn't think had anything to do with the kids. The same kind of appreciation, the same kind of intimacy, she'd seen there the night before, just as he was about to kiss her.

But they both seemed to come to their senses at once. He patted her hand and took his own away. Then they stood and got busy taking the remnants of their sandwiches to the sink to dispose of them and put the plates in the dishwasher.

''You must be beat,'' Gib said as they locked up, turned off the lights and climbed the stairs together.

But fatigue was less what Bailey was feeling than some other things that had to do with the memory of the previous evening's ending and the forbidden desire for another of those kisses they'd shared.

"How about you?" she countered. "You're up before dawn, work all day and come home to more. How do you keep up your energy?"

He laughed wryly. "It seems to be keeping itself up these days."

They reached the door to her room, but before Bailey could go into it he stopped her with a hand on her arm. A hand that set off more of those lightning bolts.

He turned her to face him as if to make sure she knew he meant what he said. "I wasn't kidding about no more nocturnal cleaning. I better not catch you up before the kids anymore. As much as I enjoyed those few minutes alone with you this morning."

She gave him a glib salute. "No nocturnal cleaning."

"And no fretting over not curing Kyle's ills with one well-turned phrase, either."

That was harder to agree to, and her grimace reflected it. "Poor little kid."

"He's thrilled to death not to have his frog living in the toilet anymore." Gib bent forward and raised an eyebrow at her. "And it's okay that you used keeping the truth from me to help ease Kyle's fears. Just don't do it with anything important."

Again she grimaced at having been found out, closing her eyes in the process this time. "I'm sorry."

But when she opened them, she found him grinning. Very nearby. "I told you, it's okay. This time."

His warning was as much teasing as anything, easing Bailey's guilt. And as they stood there together—

very close together—the pull of the attraction between them that they'd avoided downstairs tightened its hold.

Gib's features smoothed. He searched her eyes with his. And then his hand at her arm slid up in a slow, tantalizing path to her shoulder, to the side of her neck, to her nape, upward to cradle her head as his mouth lowered to hers in the rematch of that kiss she'd been craving.

Bailey told herself to put a stop to it. To step away. But how could she deny herself what she'd spent twenty-four hours wanting more of? How could she end what she was enjoying so, so much?

She couldn't. She just didn't want to.

His lips were parted, warm, only slightly moist. Savoring hers in a slow kiss that was growing deeper by the minute until his tongue finally did a tentative introduction, learning its way around the bare insides of her lips, the tips of her teeth and then her tongue.

She answered by opening her mouth a bit wider, too, inviting more, accepting more, every bit as willing as he to explore a little farther.

His hand still held her head braced against his kiss, his fingers caressed her hair, made small circles on her scalp. His other arm wrapped around her, holding her close enough for her breasts to be pressed firmly, wonderfully, to his chest, bringing her whole body up against his—soft molding to hard, curve into valley—in a perfect fit that made it seem as if they'd been carved one for the other.

She snaked her own arms under his, laid her palms to his back and feasted on the feel of that broad, hard expanse that rippled beneath his shirt. Every mound of muscle was within her reach, there for her to ride with mounting pleasure in each new one she found.

But even as she was falling more and more under the spell of his kiss, of the feel of his big body molded to hers, of her own attraction to this man, her own feelings for him, he drew the kiss to an end.

"I can't believe I did that again," he said, yet without letting go of her. Instead he laid his forehead against hers while the hand in her hair still did a sensual massage.

"It isn't what we *should* have done," she agreed, echoing his words of the previous evening but not budging herself, still savoring the feel of his well-defined back.

Her words seemed to mobilize him, though. Gib drew a long breath, sighed it out and released her—slowly, reluctantly, but completely.

"I'll see you tomorrow night," he said then, as if he was in a hurry to put some distance between them. As if that would make them both stronger, more resistant to the temptation they seemed to share.

Bailey nodded and went into her room, closing the door even though he was still standing there because she knew that if she left it open she might give in to what she really wanted and slip back into his arms.

But it was a while before she heard Gib move from that spot.

A while before she could step any farther back herself.

A while before she felt sure that thin wood panel was going to be enough to keep them apart.

When she finally heard Gib go into his own room, her heart was still racing, her skin was still tingling, her blood was still running hot and fast from that kiss, from all the man could do to her with a simple glance, a single touch.

And even though she knew without a doubt that it was a mistake, she couldn't help wishing he'd come through that door at any minute and start where they'd left off.

Chapter Seven

Kyle, Kate and Evie had a play group at the recreation center Friday morning. After her experience getting all three kids to the mall the day before, Bailey knew to allow plenty of time so she wouldn't be late to the eleven o'clock session they were signed up to attend.

She was looking forward to it. According to Gib, there were separate activities for each age group, and all she'd have to do was sit in the bleachers of the gymnasium during the hour the kids would be occupied.

It sounded like bliss—a whole hour without anything to do.

The rec center was only a few blocks from the house. A squat blond brick building, it housed an ice-skating rink, the gym and several smaller rooms to accommodate the adult-education and crafts classes held there.

Bailey found the gym divided into sections where teenagers waited for their young charges, two for each group. Since this was a weekly event that had been going on all summer, Kate and Kyle knew exactly where they were supposed to go and headed for their areas as soon as Bailey took them into the gym. Evie was a different story, and Bailey had to ask for some help in finding the group for the smallest kids.

But once she had, she climbed to a midpoint on the bleachers, where mothers and a few fathers gathered in their own clusters, and took from her purse the paperback novel she'd brought along.

She'd bought the book on her way to the Hardens' house the day she'd started her job there, thinking that she'd have a lot of time to kill. After all, Marguerite always kept one handy, and frequently Bailey came home at the end of the day to find her housekeeper reading while she waited for her. She also knew that Marguerite read a book in just two or three days, so Bailey had naturally assumed there were a lot of opportunities in a housekeeper's schedule for escaping into a good book.

But so far, this was the first chance she'd had to open the cover of the one she'd chosen.

She made it only to the second page when a hurt cry rose from the ranks. It didn't sound like one of her charges, and she was surprised at herself, at the realization that she could distinguish one cry from another. But she could.

She looked up, anyway, and watched as a woman hurried from the bleachers to a little boy in Kate's group who seemed to have run into the gym wall and banged his head.

The boy was wailing to beat the band, but there was no blood or any sign that he needed more than his mother's help, so Bailey went back to her book.

She made it to the third page when she felt the bench seat jiggle slightly beneath the weight of someone sitting beside her. Close beside her.

She glanced up to find that Kate had joined her.

"Hi," Kate said very seriously.

"Is something wrong?"

"No."

That was hard to believe. Kate looked as if she was on the verge of tears.

Bailey gazed in the direction of Kate's group. The three- and four-year-olds were standing in a circle, holding hands and singing a song. Every few seconds they all kicked their right legs out or shimmied down to their haunches or jumped in the air.

"That seems like fun," she said, pointing with her chin toward the group. "Didn't you like playing it?"

Kate shrugged one tiny shoulder and stuck her thumb in her mouth.

Thinking maybe she'd missed something from before, Bailey said, "Did you get hurt when that other little boy did?"

Kate shook her head, thumb still firmly in her mouth.

"Did something happen to make you want not to be with the other kids?"

Again the silent head shake.

"Don't you feel well?"

Kate didn't answer that one at all. Instead she stared intently down at the little boy who'd been hurt. He was sitting on his mother's lap a few rows below them. His mother seemed to be trying to coax him out of sniffles that he was working hard to keep up to soothe his injured pride more than anything.

"Tha's Marky," Kate offered then. "He's my frien'."

"He'll be all right," Bailey assured her, assuming Kate was upset that he'd been hurt. "I think he just bumped his head."

"He was runnin' too fast when he wasn't spose to."

"I don't think he'll do it again."

"Tha's his mommy."

"I thought it might be."

"I used to has a mommy."

"I know you did," Bailey said, but a bit of a red flag went up in her and she suddenly hoped all she was dealing with was Kate's sympathy for her friend's bumped head.

"I don't has a mommy no more."

"I know that, too. Are you sure you don't want to go be with your group, Kate? I think they're playing Simon Says now and I'd hate to see you miss it. I'll bet you'd like it."

Kate's gaze didn't shift from the scene below them, and there was something in her eyes that broke Bailey's heart. A yearning. A hunger.

"I miss my mommy," Kate announced then.

A wave of fresh uncertainty rose up in Bailey, and she wished, as she had the day before, that she wasn't at such a loss with everything that involved these kids. "I'm sure you do," she said, feeling her way as she went along. "Do you remember a lot about your mother?"

"I memember that she usta let me sit on her lap lots of times. An' she smelleded good."

"Those are nice things to think about. I lost my mom about a year ago, and sometimes I can still smell the perfume she wore, too."

Kate looked up at her. "Where'd you lose her?"

Oh, I really am bad at this, Bailey thought. "That's a way of saying she died. Like your mom."

"In a cars crash?"

"No, my mom had a different kind of an accident."

"What kind?"

Should she try to explain to a small child that the old furnace in her parents' house had had a carbon-monoxide leak that had silently killed both her parents in their sleep?

She didn't know. But she also didn't know what else to do, so she told Kate as simply as she could, leaving out the name of the gas so the big words didn't confuse her, and fretting the whole time that she might be frightening the little girl by telling her a story in which people went to sleep in their own bed, in their own house, and died.

She was relieved that when she'd finished Kate didn't seem upset. The child just nodded very solemnly, as if she understood and commiserated.

Then Kate said, "It's not very nice, is it?"

"To lose your mom and dad? No, it isn't. It isn't very nice at all." And maybe that tragedy, that terrible hole that had been left in her own life was part of why she wanted so badly to start a family of her own now. To have a child.

"When do you think our mommies and daddies'll come back?"

Bailey's stomach knotted like a hard fist, and again she was unsure what to say. She settled on the truth. "They won't come back, honey."

"Not never?"

"I'm afraid not."

"Oh."

Kate stuck her thumb in her mouth again, stared down at the little boy she'd called Marky and seemed even more dejected.

Bailey suddenly wished she could call back the words that she thought must have been the wrong thing to say.

But what else could she have said? She couldn't have let Kate believe her parents were going to come back. Surely in the time since the accident, Kate had been talked to about death and what it meant. This couldn't be news to her, could it?

But even if it wasn't news to her, Bailey felt sure there were better ways to deal with it. She was just so clumsy at every turn with these kids. And she didn't know why.

She wanted to believe it wasn't that she was bad at this role she'd taken on, that it was just that Kyle and Kate carried unusual baggage and were in an unusual situation.

But even though that might be true, she couldn't let herself off the hook so easily. A child of her own through artificial insemination would end up in an unusual situation. And that child would have sad, fearful moments. That child would have questions about who its father was, where its father was. That child would no doubt have a craving for that missing parent, just the way Kate was craving a mother.

And if Bailey couldn't deal with Kate's and Kyle's questions or insecurities or fears, how could she deal with those of her own child?

It was a question she didn't have an answer for. A question she couldn't deal with when she needed to deal with the immediate problem of Kate's questions and insecurities and fears because the little girl was staring up at her again with big green eyes.

"Would *you* be my mommy?"

Bailey's heart broke all over again and still she was unsure how to handle this. "There isn't anything I'd like better than to be your mommy, honey. But I'm afraid it doesn't work like that."

"How do's it work?"

"Oh, your uncle Gib will need to find a lady he loves and marry her, and then she'll be your mom." And Bailey suffered a terrible rush of jealousy at that thought.

"Wha'f I don't like her and don't *want* her to be my mommy?"

"Would your uncle Gib pick someone you didn't like?" she cajoled.

"I like you."

If Kate was trying to claim ownership of Bailey's heart, she was doing a good job. "I like you, too."

"Could you be my betend mommy? For jus' a itty bitty while?"

Bailey worried that she might be misleading Kate somehow to agree to that. That she might be encouraging an attachment she shouldn't. That she might be setting the little girl up for a fall later on. Yet to deny the request was a rejection she couldn't mete out.

Treading softly, she said, "For any time I'm with you and taking care of you, I guess that's sort of what

I am—a pretend mom. As long as you know it's only pretend."

That answer didn't seem to thrill Kate, but it didn't push her back into her shell, either. Instead she said, "Then do you think I could sit in your lap?"

"Absolutely," Bailey answered without hesitation, scooping the small child up and holding her much the way Marky was being held by his mother.

Kate wiggled around until she was snuggled just so against Bailey, resting her head on Bailey's chest. When she was comfortable, she put her thumb back in her mouth and sighed a soft, resigned sigh.

Bailey kept her arm wrapped around Kate and dropped her chin to the top of the little girl's head, hoping with all she was worth that she hadn't said or done too many wrong things.

But one way or another, there was no denying that she felt the heavy weight of a responsibility she'd never expected to come with this job.

Bailey had only thrown on her sweatsuit and put a brush through her hair to take the kids to the play group in the morning. Once they were down for their naps that afternoon, she took her shower and paid real attention to her appearance.

She caught her hair on the crown of her head with a lacy elastic ruffle, twisting the ends so it was a curly topknot and let the shorter wisps feather her face and neck. Then she put on her best—and coincidentally tightest—jeans before taking out a V-neck T-shirt to wear on top.

Or maybe not.

The T-shirt was one of her favorites. It showed off her collarbone and chest to good effect, but it also occasionally dipped to bare a bit of cleavage. And she wasn't sure if wearing something even slightly enticing was a good idea after the way things were between her and Gib.

Yet she couldn't make herself hang it back in the closet once she had it down. Even though she knew she was playing with fire. But it was Friday night, after all, and somehow that seemed to call for a touch of daring.

Besides, the kids would be right there with them the whole evening. They'd be a safety net.

Until they went to bed.

But she tried not to think about that, told herself she was wearing the shirt because she liked it, because it was cool and comfortable, and that that was all there was to it.

As she was putting the finishing touches to her mascara a few minutes later, she heard the sounds of someone downstairs in the kitchen. It spurred a glance at the clock.

Since she'd had the kids already out today for the play group—and again because Friday seemed like a day for a break in routines, not to mention that Bailey had had lightening Kate's spirits in mind—she'd treated the kids to lunch at a fast-food restaurant that offered an elaborate playground and let them stay well into the afternoon. As a result, they'd gotten home and gone down for their naps later than usual, and now it was nearly four-thirty.

Thinking Gib must have come home already, Bailey finished with her mascara and headed downstairs, eager to see him and spend even a few minutes alone with him before the kids got up.

But it wasn't Gib in the kitchen doing something at the stove that filled the air with the scent of garlic and olive oil. It was another man—same height, similar build, hair the identical dark chocolate color—though cut short all over—and a killer smile he tossed over his shoulder at her when he heard her come up behind him.

"I know the doors were locked when I went upstairs. So who are you and how did you get in?" she asked amiably, doubting he was a cooking burglar and thinking it more likely he was family or friend.

"Jack Harden. I'm Gib's cousin. And I have a key."

"Jack—the third musketeer?"

The man's dark green eyes responded with delight. "He told you about me."

"Only a little. When he was talking about his brother's death."

"So he didn't tell you I always come over on Friday night and cook dinner?"

"Not a word."

"He must have had other things on his mind." Jack's gaze took in her appearance and made it clear he thought Bailey was one of those other things.

Bailey thought it was more likely the continuing saga of her household and child-care failures that had made Gib forget about his cousin.

"You're Bailey Coltrain," he went on, when she forgot to introduce herself. "I was here last Saturday when Gib interviewed you. I saw you from the window upstairs when you left."

"You're the police officer who had me checked out."

He inclined his handsome head. "And gave you an A-one rating. I want points for that."

It struck Bailey as strange that she could be standing only a few feet away from a man with looks to die for and charm to spare, and not feel the slightest bit attracted to him. In fact, all she could think about was how disappointed she was that it hadn't been Gib she'd discovered down here. Gib she was talking to at that moment. Gib who so openly flirted with her.

And she found herself torn between gratitude that she didn't have to try cooking tonight and regret that this other man would be spending the evening with them because she didn't like the idea of sharing Gib with his cousin.

But sharing Gib with his cousin wasn't exactly how the evening played out.

Rather than Jack keeping Gib from her, Jack seemed to focus on Bailey and keep her from Gib.

Not that she liked that any better, because she didn't.

Oh, it was flattering to have Gib's good-looking, funny, charismatic cousin treating her like a prize he was intent on winning. He was just the wrong man for the event.

But once Gib got home and the evening progressed, there was one thing Jack deserved credit for. He somehow changed the tone of things. Or maybe it was the effect of it being Friday night.

But either way, the time passed with a jovial mood. Lots of teasing, flirting and lightheartedness that made it fun, even if Bailey would rather have been alone with Gib.

By the time the kids were back in bed for the night and Gib, Jack and Bailey went into the living room to relax, Bailey knew Jack's game well and opted for sitting on one of the two single overstuffed chairs instead of the sofa where Jack was headed.

It was odd, because after what she thought had been a lot of overt clues to Jack that she wasn't interested, only with that did he seem to get the idea. Once she was comfortable sitting beside Gib in the other chair, she glanced up to find Jack looking from her to Gib and back to her again, only to smile in a way that conceded his loss and said let's be friends, then.

Bailey smiled back, relieved that he finally seemed to have gotten the hint and hadn't taken offense in the process.

"So tell me why you aren't involved with anyone and have never been married," Jack said, for the first time lacking any note of flirting in his voice and sounding more like someone's big brother.

"Don't be so nosy," Gib said before Bailey could answer. Then to her, "It's the cop in him."

Gib had been running interference all night, putting himself between her and his cousin or his cousin's probing questions, but this time Bailey noticed Gib didn't seem particularly enthusiastic about letting her off the hook. Nor did he change the subject so she had an easy out. It seemed clear he was curious himself and for that reason alone she decided to answer.

"I guess I've just never found much time for romance," she said, adding with some self-deprecation, "and I've been told I'm off-putting with men."

Jack raised his chin a notch as if he understood that point of view perfectly.

Gib said, "You're kidding? What idiot thought that?"

Bailey laughed, realizing that she was different here, with Gib, than she had ever been anywhere else, with any other man. Maybe it was because she felt different about him. Maybe it was because he made her feel different even about herself—more down-to-earth the way he was, more in touch with things, more vulnerable, more feminine...

Much more feminine. In fact there was something about the quietly intelligent, ruggedly gentle man that made her feel a heightened awareness of the fact that he was male—all male—and she was female.

"Come on," Jack said. "Someone who looks like you do? You must have at least come close to getting married once or twice."

Again Gib seemed even more interested than his cousin, and it was to Gib that she aimed her response. "There was one relationship a few years ago but he broke it off. I wasn't what he needed."

And that was all she could say without giving herself away. The truth was that he'd said she'd treated him like one of her patients—a few minutes to tell her his symptoms, write up a quick prescription to make things all better and that was that. He'd said there was more to him, more to his problems than she was recognizing. And that she wasn't up to the challenge.

Remembering that suddenly caused Bailey another jab of self-doubt as she wondered if the same complaint could have been filed by Kyle and Kate in the past two days. Certainly she'd felt a strong need to put a quick Band-Aid on their hurts and have that be enough. But it wasn't enough. And she didn't know what was.

"Hey—" Gib broke into her thoughts "—don't look so glum. We've all been in relationships that haven't worked out. I was in a marriage that didn't. Even Jack here—'' Gib stretched out a long leg to give his cousin a friendly kick ''—has been shot down on occasion.''

''Yeah, just look at tonight,'' Jack said with a laugh. ''I couldn't beat old Gib's time to save my life.''

Gib's second kick was less friendly. To Bailey he said, ''Don't mind him. He thinks he's funny.''

''Who's being funny?''

''Not you,'' Gib assured him.

''I like that. I come over here, cook you a pasta primavera that melts in your mouth and you insult me. I don't have to stay around here and take it, you know.''

Gib grinned. ''Okay.''

Jack laughed. ''I get it. You want me out of here so you guys can be alone. That's why you left messages on my answering machine today trying to cancel dinner tonight, isn't it?'' he countered.

Bailey had no doubt she was witnessing the two of them needling each other in a way they probably had their whole lives. Neither of them took the other seriously, but she, on the other hand, was very interested to learn that Gib had tried to keep Jack from what was a weekly date.

''If you got the messages, why'd you come?'' Gib asked with a laugh of his own.

''I didn't get them until I was already here and called home to check my machine.'' Then to Bailey he said, ''He's been making up excuses for me not to meet you all week. Very possessive, isn't he?''

He had been tonight—and it had delighted her—but she didn't know anything about the rest of the week.

"I just didn't want him coming over here to play Don Juan and get in the way," Gib explained to Bailey.

"Get in *his* way with you is more like it."

"Didn't you say something about going home?" Gib prompted.

"He's embarrassed," Jack confided to Bailey. "And fighting like hell not to admit that he thinks you're pretty terrific. You see, he has this idea that he's going to play it solo, maybe for the rest of his life. Something about no woman wanting to take on three kids who don't belong to her and him not being able to take on any more himself."

"Are you a cop or an informer?" Gib didn't sound so lighthearted anymore.

"She ought to know where you stand, don't you think?"

Gib just stared at his cousin. Glared, actually.

"Okay, so maybe it isn't my place to say it."

"No, it isn't."

"And I really should get out of here before I stick my foot in it any deeper. Right?"

Gib agreed by standing up.

"Right. I've worn out my welcome tonight," Jack said to Bailey as he stood, too, although he didn't sound too perturbed.

Even so, as Bailey followed them to the entryway, she was concerned that she'd somehow caused a rift.

But once they were there, Jack changed the subject, offering to buy Gib lunch on Monday to make amends, and Gib accepted without any rancor.

He also opened the front door and leaned his shoulder to the jamb in a stance that invited his cousin to leave, and Jack didn't waste time on long goodbyes.

When he'd gone out, Gib closed the door behind him but stayed leaning against the jamb. He pinched the bridge of his nose and shook his head, then looked directly into Bailey's eyes. "What should I apologize for first? Not warning you that Jack might show up tonight? His being in hot pursuit the whole evening? Or this last little ditty?"

Bailey laughed. "None of it was a big deal. And he's right—he makes a great pasta primavera, so he probably does deserve to be forgiven for his sins."

Gib nodded and smiled a small, chagrined smile as he reached out and took her hand in his, fiddling with her fingers. "Shall I apologize for how I acted, then?"

She hadn't seen anything wrong with the way he'd acted, either. "I don't know what for."

"Being a jealous jerk. Putting myself between you and Jack every time he seemed to be getting too close because I couldn't stand it."

No apologies were necessary for his feeling jealous or for anything he'd done, since it had all been very flattering and she'd *wanted* him between her and his cousin. "I didn't notice that you were being a jerk at all."

"I don't know how you could have missed it."

He was still intent on her fingers, caressing them, entwining them with his. Even such a small thing felt wonderful and set off sparks to dance along the surface of her skin.

But the evening's last little ditty—as he'd called it— weighed on her and she couldn't let it pass without asking about it. "Is Jack right about you thinking nobody will ever want to take on the kids and your not wanting any more?''

Gib's gaze was on their two hands, but his eyebrows did a shrug. ''Pretty much, yeah.''

''There are a lot of women who marry men with kids and raise them and are perfectly happy to do it.''

''Not in my experience.''

She knew he was referring to his ex-wife, and she could hardly take further issue with that without sounding as if she were applying for the position. So she switched to the other part of what Jack had brought up. ''I had the impression you were crazy about the kids. I'd think you'd want more.''

''More than three?'' Gib laughed as if he couldn't believe she was serious. ''I'm definitely crazy about my crew. I couldn't love them better than I do. But three kids is not a small family. You should know by now how much of a handful they are. But the bigger part of it is that I just don't think I could give any more kids the time and attention they need or deserve.''

''But wouldn't you like just one of your own?'' And why did this mean so much to her suddenly? It wasn't as if he were the candidate for fathering the baby she had planned. What difference should it make to her?

Except that it did make a difference. A big one. So big that in that moment it made her realize that she was coming to care for this man. That maybe, just maybe, she was falling in love with him. And that she just *might* want him to be her child's father.

''I don't have any burning desire to make babies of my own,'' he was saying when she refocused her attention. ''Sure, I'm curious about how I'd do, what I'd come up with. But besides not having enough time to go around, I also worry that if I were to add another kid or two of my own to the mix, Kate, Kyle and Evie might feel displaced. And I'd never do anything that might hurt them. They've had things rough enough as it is."

He tugged on her hand, pulling her to stand close in front of him, his shoulder still against the jamb, and grinned down at her. "Why are we talking about this now? Oh, I know—that's Jack's fault, too. He just threw a great big wrench into the perfectly good Friday night I had planned."

She knew he was changing the subject and she couldn't think of a way to prevent it. Besides, the evening had been a lot more fun before, and she didn't want to turn it any more serious than she already had, so she played along. "What did you have planned?"

"It was exciting stuff. Are you sure you want to hear when it's too late to do any of it?"

He was still holding her hand, but he was holding it to his chest in a way that had her even closer than she had been before. Close enough to smell the after-shave he'd put on when he'd shaved and showered after getting home tonight. Close enough to feel the warmth his big body exuded. The power.

"I'll try not to be too disappointed. What did you have in mind?"

"Succulent hot dogs cooked on the barbecue out back. A long walk through the neighborhood. Ice cream—a double dip with sprinkles—at the new place over on the next block. Steamy stuff, huh?"

"Sounds good to me." Great in fact. Better than he knew, because she would have been with him and without his cousin to distract either of them.

"Hey, don't ever let it be said I don't know how to show a girl a good time."

"Not me. I'd never say that."

His eyes searched hers, their green flecks darkening as his face eased into a more sober expression for a moment. Then he sighed and smiled a bit ruefully. "Oh, I'm in trouble here. Big, big trouble."

"Why is that?"

He didn't answer her. He just dipped down and kissed her, lightly, playfully, sweetly.

But it was enough. More than enough to chase away all her own qualms, all her own reasoning and rationalizing and knowing better. Bailey kissed him back.

She let her free arm slide around him just the way his went around her, and she let her head fall back so he could have his way with her mouth. He deepened the kiss, parting her lips so his tongue could come to explore, to tease, to teach and torment so deliciously that she couldn't think of anything but how much she liked it, how to match him, tantalize and tease him, too.

So what if this was forbidden fruit? She had to have her fill. She just had to.

Gib released the hand he held to his chest so he could cup the back of her head in his big palm, and Bailey laid hers along the corded side of his neck, savoring the feel of his skin above the banded collar of the shirt he wore. There was no place she'd rather be than in his arms, pressed to the length of him the way she was at that moment.

His hand dropped down her back, and those long, thick, strong fingers of his began a massage that meshed them with her flesh and felt so good that it turned her insides to jelly.

But even as a soft moan rolled in her throat, she had visions of other spots on her body being tended to that way and a fierce craving for it urged her to writhe gently against him. Gib must have noticed—or maybe just felt more welcome—to pull her shirt from the waistband of her jeans and slip his hands underneath.

Deft, callused hands that kneaded her back and left her pliant to his every whim, swaying with the ebb and flow of his caress, wishing for it—willing it—to move around front...

And when he did, when he'd loosened her bra and closed those magic hands over her bare breasts, it felt so incredible that she couldn't go on kissing him. Her head fell back and a moan of pure wonder joined the sigh that escaped her lips.

Gib kissed her chin, her jawbone, her earlobe and worked his way down to the side of her neck, the hollow of her throat.

She felt only the tip of his tongue trace the lines of her collarbone, the V of her T-shirt, all the while his hands encased her breasts, teased her nipples into tight, hardened kernels, set off flames inside her that licked lower, lower, lighting a desire for more. For clothes to be shed. For the feel of his hard, naked body against her own. For his hands to move across every inch of her flesh, to find that spot between her legs that wanted so, so badly to meet him, open to him, encase him....

But suddenly, into thoughts of getting as close to him as a man and a woman could be, came other thoughts. Thoughts about his being satisfied with the family he already had. About how she wanted a child more than anything in the world. Thoughts about all

the rest of what he didn't know about her, too, because she hadn't been honest with him. And suddenly, in her mind, a chasm opened up between them
that, at that moment, she couldn't cross.

"I can't do this. Not now," she forced herself to
say, even though her body was crying out for him to
go on.

Gib's hands went around to her back again, and he
raised up from where he'd been kissing his way nearer
to her cleavage. He dropped his forehead to hers.

"The kids are asleep," he reminded her in a voice
that was raspy with desire, guessing her reason.

"It isn't that. There are just...things...you should
know before we... But not now..."

He didn't say anything for a moment. Maybe he was
waiting for her to tell him those things, after all. But
when she didn't, he said, "Okay. Whenever you're
ready."

She was ready right then. Ready for him to make
love to her. But she wasn't ready to just blurt out so
many of the other secrets she'd kept.

"Another time. Another time," she whispered.

He took his hands out from under her shirt and
kissed her nose. "Okay," he repeated.

But he didn't let her go, and she knew that if she
stayed there in his arms her resolve was going to melt,
so she slipped away from him. "Maybe tomorrow..."

He inclined his handsome head, letting her know he
wouldn't push her, not to make love and not to tell him
what she had to tell him, either. All he said was, "I
guess I'll see you in the morning, then."

Still she hesitated, tempted to do a full confession,
throw herself on his mercy and hope they still ended

up in his bed. But she didn't do it. Instead she said good-night and put every ounce of willpower into heading for the stairs.

"Jack's wrong, you know," Gib said to her back.

She paused on the second step to look over her shoulder at him. "About what?"

"About me not admitting how terrific you are."

She could only hope he still felt that way when he learned all of what she had to tell him about herself.

But there he was, leaning against the jamb again, his arms crossed over his chest, tall, muscled and oh-so-good-looking, and she just couldn't do it, any more than she could give in to the urge to throw caution to the wind and run back to him.

So instead she repeated her good-night and went the rest of the way up those stairs, thinking the whole time that, yes, maybe tomorrow she would tell him everything....

Until she remembered that to tell him everything could well mean the end.

Chapter Eight

Bright and early Saturday morning, the kids were packed off to their grandparents' house. Once they were out of the way, Bailey and Gib began a day of marathon housecleaning that taught her a great deal about how to perform the various chores.

It also taught her that housecleaning was not her favorite pastime, even when she could concentrate on it and do it right.

On the other hand, housecleaning with Gib was something she might forfeit a vacation in the Bahamas for. And that fact made her realize just how far gone she was.

Dirt, dust, grime and even the gunky mess left by Kate and Kyle who'd used soda crackers as sailboats in Kyle's bathtub the night before were secondary to Bailey's pleasure in spending the day alone with Gib, working side by side.

He had a knack for turning even the most distasteful duty into an enjoyable experience by peppering it with wit, charm and humor. There was no arrogance about him, none of the conceit, self-centeredness or self-importance she so often ran into in the men she usually encountered.

It also didn't hurt that watching him was a treat all in itself.

Temperatures outside were in the nineties, so he was dressed to keep cool—a pair of cutoff jeans shorts and a white tank top with armholes cut into deep enough scoops to leave the sides of his chest tantalizingly bare, not to mention shoulders and well-muscled biceps that were perfectly carved specimens. Add to that long, strong, powerful legs with just a smattering of hair, and Bailey's stomach fluttered every time she stole a peek at him.

Plus there was something about how capable he was at everything that was pretty attractive, too. And the agility of his big hands made her mind wander back to the previous evening and remember the feel of them against her bare skin, on her breasts.

There just wasn't anything about the man that she didn't like, and so even cleaning cobwebs out of corners turned into a not unpleasant task when it meant being with him. Or watching Gib's taut, lean body stretch out nearly to the ceiling to reach them.

Not that he did all the work while Bailey ogled him. She did her fair share of washing windows, scrubbing baseboards, sponging down walls. Of climbing, crawling and craning to clean. Of expending more energy than she'd ever known she possessed.

The trouble was, all the energy she expended was physical, and even the bone weariness that crept in as

the day went on didn't wear out the sexual energy
generated between them. In fact, the sexual energy
only seemed to increase, so that by five that afternoon when they finally finished and wilted onto the
couch with glasses of iced tea, she still couldn't help
contemplating what it would be like to make love with
him right there and then.

Maybe what she needed was a cold shower rather
than a cold drink, she thought. Because as Gib raised
his legs to the coffee table, rested his head back against
the sofa cushions and pressed his glass against the side
of his thick, damp neck, all she could think about was
that she wanted to be that glass, grasped in his hand,
held to his bare skin.

And he didn't help the situation when he used his
other hand to rub the sweat off his slightly hairy chest
where it was exposed in the deep U neckline of the
tank top. Instead she considered volunteering for the
job of wiping him down with her own hands.

No, physical exhaustion was no antidote for what
ailed her. On the contrary, it seemed to weaken her
resistance, to peel away every ounce of reason and re-
straint, and reduce her to a completely elemental,
sensual frame of mind.

Luckily, Gib seemed just plain tired and not on the
same wavelength, so she looked away from him to as-
sess the fruits of their labors and drink her tea.

"How long do you think it'll take the kids to come
in here and tear the place apart again?" she asked to
make conversation and distract herself.

Gib laughed ruefully. "Let's see...when I dropped
them off this morning, my folks said they'd bring
them back tomorrow night about seven. I'd give them

maybe until seven-thirty to have the whole house turned upside down. If we're lucky.''

"Ah, a full twenty-six hours of clean and orderly."

"Enjoy it while it lasts."

Gib reached over and squeezed her knee affectionately, and Bailey had to fight to keep from groaning at the tingling sensations even nothing more than a friendly touch set off in her.

"You worked above and beyond the call of duty today," he said then.

This time Bailey laughed. "I don't think so. I made half the messes this week and house*cleaning* is what you hired me to do, remember? I think it's you who went above and beyond the call of duty."

"That's true," he said, as if he'd been taken unfair advantage of and just realized it. "I should have spent the whole day sitting here with a beer, watching you work. You owe me."

The teasing tone that had started the night before under Jack's influence had carried through the day, and so Bailey knew he wasn't serious. "What would you like to exact as payment?"

"Ooo, you're leaving yourself wide open here. Very dangerous."

Probably not as dangerous as the things that were going through her mind. "Okay, I reserve the right to judge if the price is too steep. What do you want me to do? Mow the grass? Wash the truck and the station wagon? Paint the porch? What?"

"Worse. Much, much worse."

His tone was so lascivious that it caused goose bumps to erupt on her skin. Still, she played along. "Uh-oh. You want me to single-handedly clean out your garage—including that high shelf where Kate thinks bats live."

"She could be right. But no, not that, either. I was thinking more along the lines of the two of us getting all spruced up like real live adults and going out to a restaurant with menus completely free of clowns or teddy bear faces so I could buy you an elegant dinner."

No doubt about it, she *really* liked this man. "*I* owe *you,* so *you're* going to buy *me* dinner?"

"An *elegant* dinner. Without a kid or a toy in sight. Wearing clothes that don't have to be spit- or spill-proof."

"Wow. You really do exact a high price for your services."

"Hey, did you think I come cheap? Now. Are you going to pay up?"

"One problem."

"Hedging on your debts, huh?"

"No, I just didn't bring any elegant dinner clothes with me."

"So we'll shower and I'll dress here, we'll go to your place and you can throw something on, then we'll go to dinner. That's the other part of this—no rushing to get it done so we can be home for a baby's bedtime. We might even stay out as late as nine o'clock."

"I don't know about that. You could be pushing it."

He wiggled one eyebrow as if he were the devil offering Eve the apple. "What do you say?"

She certainly didn't have to think about it, but in the spirit of the game she pretended to. "I suppose. If you're going to twist my arm."

"Ever been to Briarwood in Golden?"

"I've only heard about it. Good things."

"Then why don't you go upstairs and have your shower—or a long, luxurious bubble bath, if that's what your heart desires—and I'll see if I can finagle a reservation."

"My place is on the other side of town, you know," she warned, resisting the lure of the bubble bath because it would take too long and postpone their evening by more than she was willing to sacrifice.

"Ah, I forgot one stipulation in this deal—I get to drive your Jag. Which means I don't mind if we have to go to Wyoming and back as long as I'm behind the wheel."

"It needs to be run, anyway. It's been sitting all week."

"So we're on?"

"We're on."

And never in her whole life had anticipation of a date—and there was no denying that that's what they'd just agreed to—thrilled her more.

Bailey's condominium was in Cherry Creek—a high-rent area nuzzled up to the southeast corner of downtown Denver. The condo itself was one of six walk-ups in a graystone building of modern design.

She couldn't help noticing that it looked a tad industrial as she and Gib went in.

She'd always liked the stark, clean lines and long, thin windows before. It had seemed stylish, contemporary, unique. But for some reason, after just a week in Gib's place, hers struck her as cold, austere and pretentious.

Sure it was neat, clean, bare of any clutter and free of the toys and other kids' things that were evident in his house even after the marathon cleaning, but still cold, austere and pretentious nevertheless.

"Very nice," Gib said, as she let them in. He tipped his head back to look up at the skylight three floors above and the railings of the other two levels that opened onto the entranceway like observation decks.

It was very nice, Bailey knew. She'd paid a fortune for it. Another fortune to have it professionally decorated. Another fortune for the original artwork on the walls. It just wasn't very homey.

Somehow she'd never noticed it before. But suddenly the thought of bringing a child into the blindingly white-on-white environment seemed almost funny. At the very least it was foolhardy—something she hadn't realized until just then.

But Bailey didn't want to think about that and ruin her pleasure in the evening that stretched out before her, so she pushed the thought aside.

"I'll just be a minute. Make yourself at home," she said, pointing straight ahead at the sunken living room as she went up the stairs, knowing her medical books, journals and magazines were safely out of Gib's sight in the den.

She'd decided what she was going to wear on the way over, so she kicked off her shoes the minute she hit the plush white carpet of her bedroom and headed directly for the closet. It was nearly as large as her whole room at Gib's house. But Bailey wasn't much of a clotheshorse, so it was hardly half full.

She chose a plain black dress she'd never worn before but knew fitted her like a second skin. It had been an impulse buy for a New Year's Eve party she'd ended up not going to because she hadn't had a date.

The dress had three spaghetti straps over each shoulder, a straight-across neckline with just a slight cut right at the center point and a hem that hit a full four inches above her knees. Sheer black nylons eased the shock of the minilength, and since Gib was so tall she opted for a pair of three-inch high heels.

Around her neck she wore a choker of four strands of pearls, and a matching pearl barrette held back one side of her hair to give her usual bob a dressier lift.

A dab of lipstick that was slightly darker than what she'd brought with her to Gib's, a spritz of very expensive perfume Jean had given her for Christmas and she was ready.

Downstairs again, she found Gib right where she'd directed him to go—the living room. He looked every bit as good dressed in a suit as he did in his jeans and work shirts. In fact, despite marveling at her first sight of him in his suit earlier at his house, she was struck all over again that he was knock-'em-dead gorgeous in a gray pinstripe with a pale dove gray shirt and a charcoal-colored tie to pull it all together.

"That didn't take long, did it?" she said to announce herself.

He was standing at her piano, where all of her family pictures were displayed, his hands in his pockets, his hip out at a sexy angle.

As he glanced from his study of the photographs to her, his eyebrows shot up appreciatively. "It would have been worth the wait if it had taken hours. Wow!"

She did a scant curtsy and inclined her head in thanks. Then she joined him beside the black baby grand.

"And you smell incredible, too," he said, closing his eyes for a moment as if he were savoring the scent.

"Better than pine cleaner?" Which was what she'd smelled of before her shower.

"Much better." His eyes were open again, and he nodded at the piano. "Do you play?"

"I used to. As a kid. My father taught me in order to build good manual dexterity." Something he had said she'd need if she ever decided to be a surgeon. But Bailey didn't add that. "I haven't played a single note in years and years, though."

Gib's gaze returned to the pictures. It was quite a gallery. There were a large number of them that chronicled her childhood and the momentous occasions growing up, some formal and informal ones of her parents, several travel photos from everywhere she'd been, a few of Jean and Jean's family.

But it was those in which Bailey posed in cap and gown that drew Gib's finger to point them out. "*Three* graduations?"

"High school, college . . . and graduate school."

"You look awfully young in that first one."

"Seventeen. I skipped a grade. And I didn't take summers off in college, so I finished that by the time I was twenty."

He arched his eyebrows again. "And graduate school? Chemistry was a graduate degree and you still didn't use it?"

Of course she couldn't correct him and let him know her bachelor's degree was in chemistry because then she'd have to explain that her graduate degree had been from medical school. So she only said, "I told you my family was big on academics."

"I must have the most highly educated housekeeper and nanny in the world."

"A lot of good it's done you, considering how this week has gone," she answered wryly, hating that she wasn't being altogether candid with him but still dragging her feet about telling him the truth in spite of the intentions she'd gone to bed with the night before.

"You're catching on quick," he assured her about the housework. "And I'm willing to stick with you while you learn. If, uh, you'll stick with me."

There was a question in his tone and when his eyes did a quick circle of the living room with its high ceiling, four sofas squared around a central glass-enclosed gas fireplace that would burn like a campfire, antique vases on marble display pedestals and several of her favorite paintings, Bailey could see that Gib was wondering all over again if her taking the job was just a lark, what other reason there could possibly be for someone who could afford so much to be working for him, and if she'd really stay.

Which of course she didn't plan to.

And suddenly she felt as if that fact was so glaringly evident that it might as well have been tattooed across her forehead for him to see.

But he didn't push it, and then she wondered if maybe her guilty conscience was just making her imagine things, because it was definitely niggling at her. More and more as time went by.

"Would you like a drink? Or a glass of wine? Or should we head to the restaurant?" she asked, to remind herself that this evening was meant to be pleasant and purely social.

He checked his watch. "I think we'd better head to the restaurant."

Bailey was relieved by his choice. She felt too exposed here. And even more of a fraud. Besides, what was between them didn't seem to fit in these surroundings. The easy rapport, the relaxed teasing, the playfulness all felt stifled and out of place. And Bailey didn't like that. She didn't like anything that altered what she had come to enjoy so much in this past week with him.

She led the way to the front door, opened it and went out into the warmth of the summer sunset.

Gib followed behind, but she caught him glancing back inside before he closed the door after them, as if he couldn't quite believe what he'd seen.

Wanting to distract him once they were in the car again, she said, "I heard you call and check on the kids before we left your house. How are they doing?"

Gib started the engine, savored the purr of it the way he'd savored her perfume such a short time before, then put it into gear and eased away from the curb. "They're having a ball. My folks spoil them rotten. Their excuse is that Kate, Kyle and Evie are the only grandchildren they'll ever have, so they go all-out. Toys, clothes, junk food, money, candy—you name it and they'll have done it, eaten it or they'll come home with it tomorrow night."

The only grandchildren they'll ever have. "Sounds like every kid's dream of a weekend with grandparents," Bailey commented but couldn't help dwelling on what he'd said. "So even your parents know you've put the old kibosh on any more children in your life?"

"My mother is a world champion matchmaker. I had to let her know where I stand."

"Do your mother and father agree with it?"

"They can see my point about three kids being a long way for my time and efforts to be stretched. But my mother is still convinced she can find a woman who'd be thrilled to take us on without adding any of her own children." Gib glanced at her. "How about you?"

"How about me?" she repeated dimly, thinking fleetingly that he might be asking her to be that woman and suffering a terrible urge to throw caution to the wind to agree to anything just to be with him.

"I know you don't have any kids now. But where do you stand on having them in your future?"

It didn't sound like a simple conversational question. It sounded more probing than that. More intent. As if the answer were very important to him.

"I agree with your mother—in fact, I know it wouldn't be hard for me personally to take on Kate, Kyle and Evie because I'm already nuts about them," she ventured.

A small, secret smile flashed across his face. "And would they be enough for you?"

Harder question. But she couldn't lie to him. Not about this.

"No, they wouldn't. I guess you could say that having at least one child of my own is my biggest priority right now."

That sobered him considerably.

"I'm not sure even I understand why it's so important to me all of a sudden," she went on, as if she could change his mind by making a good enough case. "Maybe it has to do with losing my parents. With not having another blood relative on the face of the earth. With wanting to see my mother and father again in my own child's face. I only know that I'm so hungry for the actual experience of carrying a baby, of giving birth, that I think about it almost constantly.'' Except this week when she'd thought about Gib even more.

He was frowning now as he took his eyes off the road to look at her for a moment. ''I wouldn't have guessed that about you. Especially not after seeing your condominium tonight.''

Bailey laughed a little. ''I know. It's a long way from kid-proof. But this whole thing has come over me just in the past year or so.''

''So you answered my ad to prepare yourself. Well, that explains some things, doesn't it?''

Bailey felt the strongest craving to explain even more. To be completely honest with him now that she'd come this far.

But if she did, if she confessed that she was only going to be his housekeeper and nanny for a few months before she went back to her real life, he might end everything right there and then. And she couldn't stand the thought of anything cutting her time with Gib short. Shorter than it already was. Especially not tonight. When being with him the way they were seemed very precious to her.

And realizing just how precious made Bailey realize something else, too—that her feelings for Gib were deep. That she might be in love with him.

Oh, she didn't want to be!

Not when on this most important point, she and Gib were fathoms apart.

But there it was.

And why, tonight of all nights, did she have to see it all so clearly?

She glanced at Gib and found his expression as disturbed as she felt. Were similar things going through his mind?

But here they were, all dressed up, alone, on their way to one of Denver's finest restaurants, and it was hard to believe what separated them was real. Especially when one look at his perfect, ruggedly handsome profile was enough to set her heart aflutter.

"Hey," she said, "how did we get into all of this? I thought I was paying my debt to you with a nice, carefree night on the town?"

She watched his features smooth into a one-sided grin. "Is that the only reason you're here? To repay your debt?" he asked, pretending to be crushed by the possibility.

"Well, yes," she joked back. "What other reason would there be?"

"My pure animal magnetism?"

"Is it pure?"

He laughed and the deep, rich sound swept her up to a higher level and left behind all her darker ruminations.

"Every now and then," he said, "I think you could be a very wicked woman."

"Who, me?"

"Oh, yeah, you," he confirmed with a sidelong glance at her. Then he joined in the attempt to bring the evening back to the level it had started out on. "Tell me about all those pictures of you on your piano. Where were you mountain climbing?"

"The Alps."

"Surfing?"

"Hawaii."

"And you were standing under the Eiffel Tower and in front of the Arc de Triomphe. Let me guess—the picture of you stomping grapes was taken in Italy?"

"It was. And I've seen the running of the bulls in Pamplona, toured castles in England, danced a genuine jig in Ireland, and gotten smashed on ouzo in Greece."

"Is there anything you *haven't* done?"

Had a baby. But she didn't say that. She said, "Learned how to cook a casserole?"

He laughed again. "Or how to cook anything else, as far as I can tell. And the man and woman with you in most of the photographs?"

"My parents. We toured Europe together about seven years ago." Just before she opened her ob/gyn practice. It had been her last hurrah before she got down to business.

"You're a strange lady."

"Am I? Strange good or strange bad?"

The smile he tossed over to her was sweet and sexy at the same time. "Strange good. Only good. And maybe strange is not the right word. Just full of surprises. Not ever what I expect you to be."

If only you knew...

But his smile, the intimate tone of his voice, brushed across her like a warm breeze on chilled skin, and for a moment she was lost in just looking at him.

Then it came to her attention that they'd arrived at the quaint old house that was the Briarwood Inn and Gib was pulling up to the front where a valet waited to take the car.

Gib got out and handed the valet the keys, then came around to Bailey's side to open her door and hold out a hand for her to take.

She didn't hesitate. Actually, she hoped her eagerness didn't show as she slipped her hand into his bigger one and relished the sensation of it closing around hers.

She also hoped he'd keep hold of it. But he didn't. He did the next best thing—he placed it in the crook of his arm and then held it there, so not only did she get to keep his hand but she got to feel the play of his muscular arm beneath her own.

Inside they were led to a table in what looked to have once been a stately library, sitting beside walnut French doors that allowed them a view of the open countryside that surrounded the place, and beyond that, of city lights just coming on for the night.

Dinner was definitely elegant as they enjoyed the shrimp, cheeses, pâté, and mousseline that the hors d'oeuvre tray offered. Then came caesar salads and after that the most delectable chateaubriand Bailey had ever tasted.

Still, in her mind, the exquisite meal paled in comparison to the man sitting across from her. He entertained her with stories of the year he'd tested his mettle by living in the Alaskan wilderness, gave her some insight into his creative side and how that had combined with his love of the outdoors and working with his hands to spur him into construction work. He teased her, he flattered her, he made her laugh and left her wondering just how many fathoms really did separate them, how many there could really be when everything between them was so good, so compatible, so much fun.

Then, with her stomach full, her body weighted with the effects of the day's work and her head a bit light from the wine she'd had with dinner, Gib drove home while Bailey rested her head against the back of the seat and stared up through the open sunroof at the star-dusted night sky.

"Tired?" he asked.

She turned just her head to look at him. "Mmm," she confirmed, yet it wasn't sleep that was on her mind. It was Gib.

She might be physically weary but sensually she was wide awake. And very, very aware of the man beside her.

Every breath he took seemed to match hers. Or maybe it was hers that were matching his. She was alert to every movement of his hands on the steering wheel, on the gear knob, each one seeming more masculinely graceful than the one before.

She loved the way he looked driving her car. He sat straight in the leather seat that could have been specially made for him, the way it fitted his big body so well. And he was in command, in control of the automobile, obviously enjoying it, coaxing the engine to give him the best it could, to build the most speed before he allowed it a quick, succinct shift into a higher gear.

Under his guidance, the Jaguar purred and performed the way it never had for Bailey, and she began to think of it as female, responding to Gib's very male ministrations.

Or was it just that she was projecting the way she might respond to them? Because the farther they got away from the restaurant, the more she was craving the feel of those masterful hands herself. And it didn't help that she kept remembering that they were going to be alone in the house tonight. Or that the air around them seemed charged with a new closeness, with more of the sexual energy they unwittingly generated.

It seemed as if Gib's mind was on the same thing, because just then he said, "You know, tomorrow is your day off. I could take you back to your place and catch a cab home if you want to sleep in your own bed tonight, have Sunday to yourself..."

It was about the last thing in the world she wanted. And she hoped the reluctant tone of his voice meant it was the last thing he wanted, too.

But she had to be sure.

"Would you rather that's what I did? Go back to my condominium for tonight and tomorrow?"

He glanced at her. His eyes seemed to draw her to him, even though the distance between them didn't change. "No, I wouldn't rather that's what you did. I'd rather take you home with me. This is probably going to sound crazy, but my place is where it feels like you belong."

It might have sounded crazy to anyone else—especially after such a short time living in his house—but to Bailey it made perfect sense because she had the same feeling.

"I'd rather go home with you, too," she answered.

That's all it took for him to ease the car onto a nearby exit ramp in the direction of his house.

His house. Where ordinarily there were three kids. All the family he wanted...

"What are we doing?" Bailey wondered in a whisper that was more to herself than to him.

But the week together, the evening, had somehow put them so in tune with each other that he not only heard but understood.

"Maybe we're giving in to what's been building up since the first time we set eyes on each other, whether we fight it or not. Whether everything is in line or not."

"But should we?"

He turned onto his street and rolled up to the curb in front of his place. "Not if you don't want to. If you aren't ready. Then we'll shake hands at the door, go up to our separate rooms and lock ourselves in until it's safe to come out again."

He said that with a smile that was too great-looking, too warm and wonderful not to return. But *should* she do more than shake his hand at the door and go upstairs to lock herself in her room?

Maybe she shouldn't.

Except that she knew she had to.

It suddenly seemed as if meeting Gib, as if every minute of this week together, had been nothing more than the lead-up to this moment because this moment was meant to be. And she didn't have the wherewithal or the desire to stop it. To stop what was happening between them.

Gib got out of the car and came around to her side to open the door. Only this time when he held out his hand to her, she knew he wasn't simply offering it because he was courteous.

She hesitated a brief moment, wondering a little about what would happen after tonight. But at that moment it didn't matter. Nothing mattered but Gib, being with him, actually learning what she'd only been fantasizing about since the day she'd met him, what she wanted too much for anything else to make any difference.

She slipped her hand into his and held on tight.

The house was dark, and once Gib had let them into it, he left it that way. He tossed her car keys and his house keys onto the table beside the staircase, shrugged his tie loose and still held on to her hand as if to let it go might make her change her mind.

It wouldn't have. Because somewhere deep inside, Bailey felt the kind of peace that comes with knowing something is right, natural, destined, and giving in to it.

He led her upstairs to his room—the largest and most uncluttered in the house. If he didn't clean it himself, she wouldn't have minded doing it just so she could take in the scent of his after-shave that lingered in the air.

The drapes of each of the two windows were open, spilling moonlight inside to bathe them in its soft glow where they stood beside the bed. Still holding her hand, Gib swung her around to face him and raised his other palm to lie along the side of her face as he searched her eyes with his.

"Last night—"

She stopped the words with two fingers to his lips, knowing he was remembering that she'd backed out of this the previous evening. Bailey just shook her head, removed her fingers and replaced them with a soft, tentative kiss.

"You're sure," he asked anyway, when it ended.

"I'm sure."

He smiled, and that alone was enough to make her heart catch. "Me too," he said, just before he kissed her, softly but not tentatively, and only then did he let go of her hand to wrap his arms around her, to pull her close up against him.

Bailey slid her arms under Gib's suit coat and laid her palms on his back, filling them with the wide expanse of solid-packed muscle as he deepened the kiss.

His tongue plunged into her mouth, teased, tormented, turned round and round in a game that began at a leisurely pace but grew more intense with each passing moment, even as he took his hands away to dispose of his coat and tie.

Bailey was only too happy to have them gone. In fact it would have been fine with her to be free of all the barriers that kept them apart.

Again Gib must have been of like mind, because when his hands came back to her they were on her shoulders. He eased her spaghetti straps to dangle around her arms and then reached for the zipper that ran the length of her spine.

What was good for the goose was good for the gander, she decided, and went to work on the buttons of his shirt. When she had them all undone, he helped by slipping off his shirt before he pushed down on her dress, baring only the upper rise of her breasts.

Lord, the man was a tease!

She ached for those big hands of his to find her breasts, to cup them in his callused palms, but he only traced their curves with a single middle finger in a feather-light stroke that nearly drove her wild. Goose bumps erupted on her skin and her nipples tightened in delicious anticipation.

And then he finally did what she was almost ready to beg of him—he cupped her breasts, kneaded them, worked the magic he'd only barely begun the night before.

Everything inside Bailey grew taut with pleasure, and a moan escaped her throat as she lost herself in his touch.

Her head fell away from his kiss, but he was undaunted, placing more of them along her jawline, down the arch of her neck, into the hollow of her throat, each one taking her breath away, leaving her dizzy and drenched in pleasure.

He paused just below the hollow of her throat to flick the tip of his tongue against that oh-so-tender spot, but only for a brief time. Then he moved on to kiss and tantalize with his tongue in a path that went to the crest of her shoulders, down her arms and inward again until he discovered her breast with his mouth.

Bailey must have gone a little weak-kneed with passion, but she only became aware of how much of her weight he was supporting when he lowered her to the bed. He continued to work his wonders on her breasts, wonders that freed his hands to slide her dress all the way off, taking her shoes with it.

Then he went to work on her nylons until she lay naked beneath him.

My turn, she thought from somewhere in the blissful clouds of desire. She found the fastener and zipper of his suit pants, fumbling only slightly in her eagerness to be rid of them.

She heard his shoes hit the floor as he helped the process, and then all at once he was gone from her side, standing next to the bed to shed the rest of his clothes.

Although she'd fantasized about the way he might look without them, she hadn't done him justice. If a more perfect man existed, she didn't ever need to see him because the sight of Gib was enough for her. Tall, lean, solid, perfectly proportioned, honed, hard and tan, he stood there in all his magnificence, wanting her.

Oh, yes, he definitely wanted her! It was there for her to see in a shaft of long, thick proof.

Then he came back to the bed, to her side, capturing her mouth with his, her breasts in his hands, throwing a heavy thigh across her own as if he were afraid she might escape him.

But that was the last thing Bailey had any intention of doing.

She wrapped her own arms around him to pull him as close as she could, discovering the greatness of his body.

Desire mounted, drove them to a near frenzy of exploration, of learning, of delight, until neither of them could hold back any longer.

Gib rose above her and found his place between her welcoming thighs. Carefully, slowly, he eased into her until he was completely encased in the warmth of her body.

Maybe certain people really were made for each other, Bailey thought, because she and Gib fitted together perfectly. They moved together smoothly in the ultimate dance that began as a gentle, careful thrusting and grew in urgency until passion took over. Powerful, potent passion that drove them on, faster and faster, so fast that it was as if they shed gravity to soar together, higher and higher....

Bailey burst onto the peak with Gib following close behind. She clung to him, rode with him while wave after wave lifted her up, rocked her from the inside out in an ecstasy more incredible, more exquisite than anything she'd ever known before. So incredible, so exquisite that she wanted it to go on and on, never to end.

Yet when the waves subsided to ever-lessening ripples, it felt so good to find herself held by Gib, melded to him, that she knew there was still some heaven left to her even in the aftermath.

Muscle by hard muscle, she felt him relax until he lay atop her in a weighted bliss.

Then his deep, raspy voice came to her through the moonlit darkness, wafted around her, infused her with his presence and connected them as surely as anything physical. "I don't know how it happened so soon. I don't know how it happened at all. But I'm in love with you, Bailey."

She smiled up into his so solemn, so handsome face and felt not only his words but his heart reaching out, almost touching hers in a union of feelings that matched the union of their bodies.

"I don't know how it happened, either. But I'm in love with you, too," she whispered.

And as if they'd agreed that nothing more needed to be said, he kissed her shoulder, held her close and rolled them to their sides, where, with his body still joined to hers, they both surrendered to exhaustion and slept without a single thought that anything could ever separate them.

Chapter Nine

The moment she woke up the next morning, Bailey felt a reassuring sense of fate. She and Gib were meant to be. Lying in his arms. Their legs entwined. The fingers of his right hand woven with the fingers of her left and both resting atop his chest. Her head pillowed by his shoulder in a crook that seemed carved out with her in mind.

So perfect did they fit together, so comfortable was she, so calm, so peaceful, so relaxed that it was as if they'd been sleeping together for years and years. Like two pieces of a puzzle.

And they weren't only a physical match. Bailey opened her eyes to the morning sun coming in through the open drapes and knew that Gib wasn't merely in bed with her, his naked body against hers, but that he was firmly in her heart, too.

She really, truly, honestly, loved him.

If someone had told her a week ago that it was going to happen—even with Gib as attractive as he was—she'd have recommended a psychiatric evaluation.

But here she was and it was true—she loved him. She loved his kids. And she was in a terrible mess.

O what a tangled web we weave...

Bailey's deception suddenly weighed heavily on her. Like a rock slide, pebbles of guilt had been raining down on her all week, until now the whole mountain of remorse seemed to have avalanched.

How could she lie in this man's bed, in his arms, love him, make love with him and not be honest with him?

She couldn't.

He deserved, he needed, he had the right to know who she really was, that her time here was limited, that she'd used his need for help around the house and with the kids for her own purposes.

And she had to tell him.

As soon as possible.

"Where do you think you're going?" Gib asked in a deep, gravelly morning voice when she tried to ease away from him. Then, before she managed more than a hairsbreadth of a parting, he tightened his arms around her and tucked her back where she'd been before.

"I'm sorry if I woke you."

"Don't be. I'd have hated to wake up and find you gone."

"I was going to wait for you downstairs. So we could talk."

"*Talk?*" he groaned in exaggerated disappointment.

He was rubbing her arm with the lightest of strokes, the tips of his fingers barely brushing the side of her breast. But it was enough—more than enough—to harden her nipples and soften her resolve to get out of his bed and address her dishonesty right that minute.

Yet even as her body snuggled against his, her conscience nudged her to say, "I have something I want to tell you."

He kissed the top of her head and left his lips pressed there. His breath was warm and sweet in her hair. "Do you have something to tell me that can't wait, say...an hour?" he said, as he raised his thigh until it rested up high between her legs, then he flexed the hard muscles of it against that most sensitive of spots.

"You aren't making this easy," she answered on a half-sigh, half-moan.

"Hmm. I thought we did it pretty easily the last three times. Did I miss something?"

They'd made love three times—the first glorious time and twice more during the night with short naps to rest in between.

It was tempting to ignore the course she'd just decided on. At least for a little while. Tempting to give herself one more moment of the bliss she might never know again after she told him the truth.

But there was something about the light of day, the sun coming in through those windows to shine down on her guilt, that wouldn't let her put off what she had to do.

Besides, as much as her body craved a fourth round, craved the feel of Gib inside her again, it was one thing to be carried away by the passion of the night, another thing to make love now, when all of her rationalizations had run out. When her whole heart and soul and mind might not be in it because a part of her was dreading what was to come. It seemed like cheating them both.

"How about if we shower and dress and meet downstairs so I can tell you what I need to. Then, if you're still so inclined, we can pick up where we're leaving off."

"*If* I'm so inclined?"

"You might not be, when you hear what I have to say."

He straightened his leg until it rested on the mattress once more and the titillating massage of her arm stopped, but he went on holding her tenderly, closely. "Is this about those *things* you said I should know the night before last?'

"Some of it. Some of it I told you on the way to dinner last night. About wanting to have a child."

That reminder made him lie very still, as if he'd put what separated them out of his mind until that moment. Just the way she had. As if he, too, had pretended it didn't exist and let himself be swept up in what swirled around them and tied them together instead.

"Must be pretty bad," he said quietly.

"What's bad is that I wasn't up-front with you from the beginning."

"You're married," he guessed.

"No." She even managed to laugh a little at the ominous tone in his voice. "It isn't that bad a secret to have kept. I'm just sorry I kept any secrets at all."

"You're a black widow serial killer."

"Being a black widow serial killer wouldn't be as bad as being married and not telling you?"

He pretended to think about it. "Close call. Why don't you just tell me here and now, save us the showers, the dressing and the trip downstairs so we can get on to my forgiving you?"

He said that as if he had no doubt that he would. But Bailey couldn't feel certain of it when she knew he was lying there under the influence of desire. She decided it would be much worse if the full impact of her deception hit him and turned him against her belatedly.

She couldn't bear that.

And if he asked her to get out of his life, she wanted to be dressed for it, armored, in a way. And ready to go with as much dignity as she could muster.

If it was possible for her to ever be ready to walk out of this man's life. Dignity intact or not.

"I think I should do this downstairs," she insisted.

A shower would also buy her some time to figure out just how to break it all to him in the best possible light, because lying there in his arms, feeling the honed hardness and heat of his skin against hers, wanting so badly not to ever move from that spot, she didn't have any idea how she was going to do this.

"You know, after this buildup, my imagination is going wild," he said. "Escaped convict. Bank robber. Runaway heiress to a small but oil-rich principality. Former president's mistress . . ."

Bailey laughed again. "My confession will seem like small potatoes after all that."

And yet it occurred to her just then to wonder what would happen between them if he didn't kick her out. Now that he would know the truth, now that they'd taken the last step into intimacy, things couldn't just go back to the way they'd been. And maybe, with what separated them, it couldn't go forward, either....

But she pushed the thought away as fast as it had come.

Everything might be all right. It might all work out. Somehow. It was possible, wasn't it?

She slipped out of Gib's arms, holding the sheet around her to sit on her knees out of his reach.

Then she forced a light tone of voice when she felt anything but. "Come on, humor me. If what I have to tell you doesn't strike you as *too* awful, we can spend the rest of the day..." *Making love* was what she'd almost said. But she changed it to "Any way you want."

He arched his brows at her and let his eyes rake over her toga-wrapped body in a slow gaze that heated her skin. "*Any* way I want?"

"Even if it means sitting in front of the television watching some sports event."

His oh-so-supple mouth eased into a grin. "That's not what I have in mind."

She smiled back, keeping her fingers crossed that she'd get the chance to find out what he *did* have in mind. "Hold that thought and I'll see you downstairs," she said.

Then she followed the impulse to dip down to kiss him, just once, briefly, on the lips, before she dragged the sheet with her and left him behind.

Bailey did not hurry through her shower or her dressing or combing her hair or brushing on a dab of mascara and blush because she wanted to allow herself all the time she could to come up with just the right thing to say when she confessed. Yet she still hadn't settled on anything when she finally went downstairs to meet Gib.

What *was* the best way to tell a man she'd lied to him when that man was someone she cared more about than she'd ever cared about anyone else? And how did she convince him—once she had managed to confess—that lying wasn't the norm for her? That she was usually an honest person? That she wasn't lying about that, too?

Definitely a tangled web.

She could hear him in the kitchen, running water. Probably making coffee. And her heart hurt for loving him so much.

Or maybe it hurt for loving him so much and knowing that love was complicated by so many other things.

She took a deep breath and crossed the dining room to the kitchen, telling herself to get on with this, get it over with.

He was only barely dressed—no shirt, no shoes or socks, just a pair of blue jeans that fitted him like a second skin and rode so low on his hips that his navel winked at her from above the waistband. He was freshly shaven, his hair was combed back and still slightly damp, he smelled of soap and after-shave, and all Bailey wanted to do was sidle up to him, slip her arms around his waist and lay her cheek against his chest.

Instead she tried to smile.

"You look like you're facing execution," he said after one glance at her.

So much for the smile.

Then he held up the cereal box he had in his hand. "Sustenance."

Cereal and the coffee that was beginning to drip into the pot and fill the kitchen with its wonderful smell.

If this goes badly, Bailey thought, *I'll never be able to drink coffee again without this sick feeling in my stomach.*

"Okay, I've waited long enough," Gib said. "What's the big secret?"

"Why don't we sit down at the table?"

They did, but Gib didn't seem to be taking this seriously. Which was good, she decided. Better that than making a big deal out of it. As big a deal as she was making out of it.

Not that she was embarrassed or ashamed of what she did for a living. Telling him or anyone else that she was a physician was hardly a chore. She was proud of her accomplishments. It was the deception that chafed. That was so hard to admit to, even now when the time had come and she'd prepped him.

"Spit it out," he ordered.

"Some of the things I've told you about myself aren't strictly true," she began. "And I want you to know that I wasn't happy about dealing in that sort of thing. In fact, the more I've gotten to know you, the more I've hated it."

"You're sure you aren't hiding a husband somewhere?"

"I'm sure."

"So what is it?"

First the truth, she thought, then the explanations and apologies for not having let it out in the beginning. "Well, for one, my degree in chemistry is an undergraduate degree—"

That's as far as she got.

Just then the front door burst open, and Bailey and Gib turned in that direction as Kyle ran in, shouting, "Uncle Gib! Uncle Gib! Somethin's wrong with Kate! She squeaks!"

Gib and Bailey headed out of the kitchen in time to find that fast on Kyle's heels came an older couple Bailey assumed were Gib's parents, the man carrying Evie, the woman carrying Kate as if she were holding a cracked porcelain statue together.

Both adults were pale and appeared upset. Kate's eyes were round with some fear of her own, and even Evie and Kyle had an air of anxiety to them.

"I was curling her hair," the woman said without preamble. "And I heard a squeaking sound. Coming from inside her. Her chest."

Gib took Kate from his mother, but the squeak was loud enough for Bailey to hear from her spot a few feet away. She watched the color wash out of his face as he held Kate up and put his ear to her chest.

"My God," he said. "Did you swallow something, Kate?"

"Uh-uh," the frightened child muttered, shaking her head vigorously in denial.

The squeak was rhythmic and regular, and Bailey had a pretty good idea what it might be. But before she could step in, Gib said to Kate, "Are you sick? Do you hurt somewhere? Did you fall down just before this started?"

"Uh-uh." And again the head shake.

"I asked her that before," the older woman offered. "If she had seemed sick I would have called an ambulance or taken her to the emergency room. But she's fine except for that noise coming from her."

"I don't wanna talk no more 'bout this," Kate said then, putting her thumb in her mouth as if that could end the whole thing.

"Sit her on the couch and I'll be right back," Bailey finally said.

There must have been something more commanding in her tone of voice than she'd realized, because Gib looked at her as if she'd surprised him. She didn't pause to explain herself, though. Instead she went out to her car, unlocked the trunk and took a black medical bag from it.

Here goes, she thought on the way back.

Of all the scenarios she'd imagined for breaking the news to Gib, this had not been one of them. She hated that he would find out this part of what she'd kept from him in front of an audience, without any lead-up, without any softening of the blow, with witnesses to the fact that he'd been misled, that she wasn't what he thought she was. But there was no way around it.

The family was all gathered near the sofa where Kate sat on the center cushion by the time Bailey returned. But it was Gib who her eyes sought out. She watched his gaze drop to the distinctive black leather bag that had belonged to her father at a time when house calls were not so uncommon. Then Gib looked up into her face again from beneath a deep, dark, confused frown.

"What's that?" Gib's mother asked with a nod at the satchel.

Bailey couldn't tear her eyes away from Gib's even as she answered the woman's question. "It's a medical bag."

"Why do you have it?" his mother again.

"Because I'm a doctor," Bailey said very quietly.

"Your *housekeeper* is a *doctor?*"

After a moment during which Bailey had the sense that Gib was waiting for her to say it was just a joke, he said, "I guess so."

Bailey could only hope her expression conveyed to Gib how sorry she was that he had to find out like this. But the level of confusion was so high in the room that she felt compelled to reassure them all that she knew what she was doing rather than addressing anything else right then.

"Obstetrics and gynecology are what I ordinarily do. But I can make an educated guess as to what's wrong with Kate and then we can go from there."

And for the moment it was Kate who had to take priority, so Bailey turned her attention to the little girl, silently asking Gib to reserve judgment of her until they could talk later.

"Explain it to me again. I'm not sure I understood what you think is wrong with Kate," Gib's mother asked an hour and a half later as Bailey sat in the waiting room of Jean's half of the office building they shared.

Raima Harden was a small, thin woman with short, curly white hair and eyes the same green-flecked hazel as Gib's. Gib's father—whom Gib resembled—was taking Kyle and Evie for a walk while Jean was behind closed doors examining Kate.

Gib sat away from his mother and Bailey, who had stayed to calm the woman's nerves rather than give Jean assistance she didn't need. He was in a chair off in one corner, watching Bailey but saying nearly nothing to her. She could only hope he was simply concerned for Kate or digesting the truth he'd just learned about Bailey, and not going over in his mind her many deceptions since she'd met him.

"Bailey?"

She'd forgotten to answer Raima's question and kicked herself into gear.

"It's likely Kate has mitral valve prolapse. In simple terms, the mitral valve is a part of the heart that works sort of like a parachute. It pulls up and lets blood through, then closes off again similar to the way an open parachute comes down." Bailey made a fist of one hand and cupped her other hand over it to demonstrate. "The parachute should form a tight seal. But if this condition is what Kate has, the parachute doesn't form such a tight seal. A small amount of blood escapes back through, and that's what's causing the squeak. Usually it can only be heard with a stethoscope, but Kate is so tiny there just isn't much of her to be soundproof. I saw this happen once before, on my emergency room rotation when I was an intern. Another slight little girl was brought in squeaking audibly."

"And it isn't life-threatening?" the older woman asked.

"Mitral valve prolapse doesn't mean that Kate has a diseased heart. In fact, it's not an uncommon condition and it usually isn't dangerous as long as a few precautions are taken. People live perfectly normal active lives—they just need to be given a series of antibiotics before things like dental appointments or invasive medical procedures that might introduce bacteria into the bloodstream and infect the rougher-than-normal valve."

The whole time she was giving this small lecture to Gib's mother, Bailey couldn't help being very aware peripherally of his listening, too. And watching her. Of the frown that never eased up.

Was he angry with her?

It didn't seem so.

But it wasn't as if he looked happy with her, either.

Disappointed, maybe?

She just couldn't tell.

"We're so lucky your friend is a cardiologist and she'd see Kate like this, on Sunday," Raima Harden was saying when Bailey reminded herself to pay attention again.

"Jean is a good friend," Bailey muttered.

"And your office is next door?"

"Yes."

"Dr. Oslin seems much older than you are."

"About ten years. She worked with my father a long time ago and took over his practice when he died," Bailey said distractedly, finding the courage to meet Gib's eyes with her own.

But the moment she looked directly at him, he glanced away, toward the door behind which Jean was doing an ultrasound, an X ray and an EKG on Kate.

It really didn't seem like a good sign to Bailey that he wouldn't look her in the eye, and her hope that things between them might weather this storm deflated.

Still, she reminded herself, he could just have been trying to assimilate the turn so many things had taken just this morning. But somehow she didn't think his silent study of her only when he didn't have to meet her eye to eye boded well for them.

Just then, the door to Jean's examining rooms opened and Bailey's old friend came out carrying Kate on one hip. Gib and his mother stood, nearly charging them in their eagerness for news.

But Bailey stayed back slightly, removed from the group. There was something about Gib's attitude that left her out, that made her feel less a part of his family than she had all week, and more a doctor without a claim to this case.

It was a sharp jab that couldn't have hurt her more had someone actually struck her, even though she knew it was possible the whole thing could only exist in her mind.

"I seed pi'tures of my heart!" Kate announced enthusiastically as Jean handed the little girl over to Gib.

"Bailey's diagnosis was right," Jean said. "Kate has mitral valve prolapse. A fairly mild one, from the looks of it. I'd like her to be established with a pediatric cardiologist right away, though—within this next week, if possible. In my practice I only see adults, and kids with this need to be watched as they grow. But there's no indication that there's any need for concern right now. I'll give you the name of a good doctor at Children's Hospital. In the meantime, why don't you all come in and I'll show you what Kate and I were up to. Then you can take our results with you for the new doctor to look at."

Gib's father came in the front door with Kyle and Evie at that moment, so Bailey volunteered to stay in the waiting room with them while Kate and the family followed Jean into the rear portion of the office again.

Bailey automatically scooped Evie up and sat with the toddler in her lap while Kyle perched on the arm of her chair.

"Is Kate sick?" he asked.

Bailey explained Kate's problem to him in as simple terms as she could, assuring him his sister was fine.

Still he said, "Is she gonna die like our mom and dad?"

"No, she isn't, honey. Not from this."

"From something else?" he sounded alarmed and yet again Bailey chafed at her own lack of skill in dealing with kids and not realizing how literally they took everything.

"No, no I didn't mean that," she said in a hurry to calm the fear she'd caused him. "Kate's okay. She'll go on being okay."

"But she squeaks. People shouldn't squeak."

"I know it sounds strange, but it isn't bad. What Kate has is just a difference in her heart, not anything worse than that."

"My friend Jer'my has six toes on his feet. You mean like that she's diff'rent?"

"He can walk all right, can't he?"

"Yeah. But it looks funny."

"Then yes, Kate's heart is just slightly different like that. Only you can't see it unless you're a doctor. And you won't be able to hear the squeak, either, as she gets a little bigger. Then only a doctor will be able to hear that, too, through a stethoscope."

"A doctor like you?"

She was afraid of having to explain what an obstetrician and gynecologist was, so she just said, "Yes, like me."

"If yer a doctor, why're you watchin' us 'stead of fixin' sick people?"

"It's a long story," she said with a glance in the direction Gib had just gone.

"How come you didn't tell us you was a doctor?"

"Oh, that's a long story, too."

"Are you gonna be our baby-sitter still or are you gonna be a doctor again?"

Good question.

And one she didn't end up having to answer because Jean and the Hardens came out again then.

"We're all done," Jean announced. "We aren't even squeaking anymore."

Gib handed Kate to his father, and as his mother reached for Evie he said to Bailey, "My folks are going to take the kids home for me while you show me *your* office."

It was a very pointed statement that sounded as if they'd discussed and agreed to that, when they hadn't. But at least he was looking at her again.

"Sure," she agreed, wondering if he just wanted to talk in private or if he didn't want her in his house. Ever again.

Everyone thanked Jean, who declined payment for her services, and walked out to the parking lot of the small burnt-umber-colored brick building.

Bailey and Gib stood back as his parents loaded the kids into their compact car, Jean started the engine of her minivan and they all drove off. And suddenly, Bailey and Gib were left alone in a heavy silence.

"I'm just next door," she said to break that silence, hating that she sounded overly cheerful.

Gib didn't say anything at all. Nor did a single muscle in his face move from the unreadable mask of his expression.

Bailey turned to her side of the building and unlocked the door, stepping inside to wait with her back pressed flat against the wooden panel for him to follow her.

He did, but in no hurry, as he seemed to study everything—the building, the upscale neighborhood around it, the parking lot, her car. And even when he finally came inside, his survey continued as Bailey closed the door.

He took a slow tour of the mauve-and-navy-blue waiting room. Of her receptionist's area. Of the hall that led to the examining rooms, poking his head into each one. Of her office in the rear, with its big walnut desk and credenza. Of the photographs on that desk of her parents. Of her diplomas all framed and hanging on the wall behind the big tufted desk chair.

"So," he said then, pivoting slowly to lean his forearms on top of the chair back in what looked like a fairly relaxed pose, except that his hands were in fists out in front of him. "You let me believe you had some experience in child care and housekeeping when you didn't. You let me think you were taking the job for the long haul when obviously that can't be true. You lied about the full extent of your schooling and degrees. You didn't tell me the truth about what you did before coming to work for me. Is there anything else?"

"No," Bailey said feebly from where she stood on the front side of her desk.

"Want to tell me what's going on with you?"

"I've told you a big part of it."

"Then maybe you should tell me which parts were true so I'll know them from the parts that weren't."

"What's true is that I've come to a point in my life where it's important to me to have a child of my own and I needed to know how to care for it. So I decided to get some experience beforehand. But if I had told you the truth the day you interviewed me you wouldn't have hired me?"

"Not on a bet."

"Well, that's why I didn't say any of it. I didn't *like* misleading you, but—"

"It was the only way you could use us."

He struck a blow with that one, but she couldn't tell if it was intentional or not. He seemed more disappointed, disillusioned, than angry—as he had every right to be. But hearing what she'd done put in terms of having *used* Gib and the kids—regardless of how accurate it was—cast such an ugly light on it, in any event.

"I hoped I'd figure out how to do the job you hired me for quickly," she went on, fighting back the tears that welled in her eyes. "And that when I did you'd get what you were paying for. Then, at the end of my time with you, I had every intention of helping you find a replacement and returning all your money."

"At the end of your time with me—three months."

"Yes. But I wasn't going to leave you hanging out to dry. I was going to make the transition as easy as I could to compensate you for having to go through hiring someone else again so soon."

"Transition," he repeated wryly, showing just a hint of the anger she'd been looking for.

She knew transition was too cold a word for what leaving Gib, leaving the kids, would be in reality. Ending her time with them in three months—ending it now if that was how this played out—would be harder than *transition* made it sound for her, too. A lot harder. But she was trying so hard not to break down and somehow that touch of aloofness helped.

"It was just what I vowed to myself to do to make up for *using* you to gain the experience I needed. I see now that it wasn't practical or realistic for any of us on any level. I just didn't know any other way to get—"

"What you wanted, even if it wasn't great for everyone else involved." Another glimmer of anger shone through his calm. In his tone of voice. In the sharpness of the green flecks of his eyes. In the taut, hard lines of his jaw.

"I'm sorry, Gib. I thought I'd just be doing a job for you, for the kids. I didn't think I'd get personally involved. And I've been chafing under my lies and what's really been happening all week long, if it helps any. I'm not proud of what I've done. It wasn't fair to you or Kate or Kyle or Evie. I was wrong to take on so much that I didn't have the foggiest idea how to deal with. I was wrong to mislead you, to take up a place in your lives that you thought was more permanent. Believe me, I've been learning more about how wrong I was by the day."

"But you let it go on, anyway. You let us get in deeper and deeper. You even let us go so far as to say we loved each other, for God's sake."

"I was about to tell you everything this morning."

"And then what?"

The million-dollar question. She wished she had a million-dollar answer for it.

"I don't know. Then it would have been up to you to let me go on for the rest of the three months. Or not."

He pushed off the chair with so much force that it banged into the desk. Then he took a few angry steps to the window to stare out at the courtyard she and Jean and their office staffs used for breaks, lunches and breathers.

Bailey had only the sight of his back by which to judge what was going on with him. And as terrific as that broad-shouldered straight-spined expanse looked, it was too stiff to mean anything good.

But then she didn't deserve anything good to come out of this, she told herself. Not only had she lied and misled him, but she'd been more of a burden than a help to him, she'd caused him more work and brought more chaos instead of order to his house, and cost him more money in the meals she'd ruined and those he'd ended up buying when she did.

He—and the kids—had definitely gotten the short end of the stick in this deal. And all the while he'd been patient, calm, understanding. He'd been willing to ride out her learning process because he'd believed she'd be around long enough for them to benefit from his effort. He'd done the extra work of cleaning up after her, helped straighten out the chaos she'd wreaked, even taken time he could have used in better ways to teach her how to do things right.

No, whatever he wanted to hurl at her in retribution she knew she had coming. And she wouldn't cry through it. She *wouldn't* . . .

Still, though, she couldn't help hoping against hope that his controlled anger was as bad as it was going to get. That he might yet let her go home with him for the rest of the three months. Three months she wanted badly to have with him. With the kids.

But then what? a little voice in the back of her mind echoed his question.

And the answer seemed to be that then everything between them would end, anyway.

But she didn't want to think about that. She couldn't think about that.

"So where do we go from here?" she heard herself blurt out, to drown that little voice in her own mind.

A dry, mirthless chuckle raised and lowered his shoulders in a split-second shrug before he shook his head very, very slowly. "We have to think about how this is going to turn out if it goes any further, don't we? Feelings are involved now. We aren't talking about just a job anymore."

"No, I guess we aren't."

"You don't want to raise someone else's kids, you want your own."

"I definitely want my own, but—"

"And I already have three kids who I'm not sure are getting everything they need from me because my plate is so full as it is. You aren't a housekeeper or a nanny, you're a *doctor,* for God's sake—the course of your life is set, and it's a world apart from mine."

But that wasn't an answer to what she'd asked. "So where do we go from here?" she repeated.

He didn't respond right away. And from his expression it looked as if that was because he didn't want to say the only thing he could say.

Then he shook his head again. "It's a dead end, isn't it? If you stay playing nanny and housekeeper on this lark of yours for a few more weeks until you come back to all this, the kids get more and more attached. *I* get more and more . . . attached. And then you'll be gone and everybody gets hurt." He finally turned to face her, to look her in the eye again. "Even you, I think."

She nodded just slightly in agreement. She couldn't refute most of what he said. It was true she wanted a child of her own. It was true he already had a big enough family. It was true that she'd gotten herself hurt already, that it could only get worse after a longer time with Gib, with the kids.

"You're wrong about no woman wanting to be mother to Kate, Kyle and Evie," she said, taking issue with the only thing she could take issue with. "They're great—" she swallowed hard against the lump that was suddenly in her throat "—great kids." Kids who deserved better than she'd given them, better than to come to count on a person who wouldn't be there for them after a few brief months.

Gib just watched her, his expression solemn, sad, full of regret—though Bailey didn't know if he regretted this that they were doing now or having hired her at all.

Or maybe what he regretted most was what they'd shared in the past twenty-four hours when they'd crossed the line into intimacy.

"Damn it!" he said, shaking his head. "Why the hell—" He stopped himself, started again with, "I wish—" Stopped once more and shook his head, raking his hands through his hair. "It just isn't going to work."

He made that sound so final. So definite.

Bailey drew herself up slightly taller, slightly straighter. She understood where he was coming from, that he wondered why the hell she hadn't been upfront with him so that maybe they wouldn't have gotten involved—forewarned was forearmed. That he wished things were different or maybe that they'd met at a better time in their lives.

But even thinking that didn't make her feel any better. It didn't make it hurt any less.

"I'm sorry," she repeated in a scant whisper.

"Yeah. So am I." He glanced at her degrees on the wall. Then at her. Then he shook his head yet again in a way that said he was still having trouble believing all he'd so recently found out about her.

Or maybe what he was having trouble believing was how anything that was so good could have turned out so bad. Because that's what Bailey found hard to accept.

"I have to get out of here," he said all of a sudden.

Then he was gone, and Bailey listened to his steps down the office hallway, across the waiting room, at the front door that he shut very firmly behind himself.

She expected to hear his truck engine start up right away after that and waited for it.

But it didn't happen.

And the longer it didn't happen, the more hope sprang to life that he'd come back in, that he'd tell her nothing she'd deceived him about mattered, nothing that separated them couldn't be bridged.

Only that didn't happen, either.

And finally, when she heard the truck start, she knew it wasn't going to.

That was when the full impact of what she'd done sank in.

And all she could do was fall back into one of the chairs that faced her desk and surrender to the kind of tears she hadn't cried in a long, long time.

Chapter Ten

"Gimme those! They're mine!" Kyle yelled.

"I'm jus' usin' 'em!" Kate yelled even louder.

"Gimme 'em back!"

"No! Not till I'm done!"

"Then I'm gonna took 'em back!"

"No, yer not!"

Sounds of a tussle overhead made Gib and Jack both glance at the ceiling in the living room where they were just about to watch a baseball game on television.

Then they heard Kate shout, "Now lookit what you did!"

"I didn't do it! You did it!"

Gib had just come down from upstairs and had barely had time to get himself and Jack a beer from the refrigerator when this latest argument broke out. He handed his cousin one bottle and said through clenched teeth, "Damn it! Those kids were supposed to be asleep an hour ago, and this is the third time I've had to break up a brawl tonight."

"I'll see what's going on," Jack offered.

"No, I'll do it." But when Gib set his own beer on the coffee table, it was with a bang loud enough to make Jack flinch.

On his way to the steps, Gib hollered, "I better not find either one of you out of your bed when I get up there!" But he doubted Kate or Kyle even heard him over the noise their own raised voices were making.

Following the sound of what seemed like incessant fighting the past two days, he found all three kids in the girls' room. Evie was standing in her crib oversee- ing the battle of wits, and Kate and Kyle were on op- posite sides of a jar of red poster paint that had spilled on the carpeting.

"Oh, for—" He cut off his own angry epithet. "What the hell is going on in here?"

"She sneaked in my room and stole my paints," Kyle tattled.

"I can use 'em some of the times."

"No, you can't!"

"I wanted to make a pi'ture for Bailey."

"Bay-we?" Evie parroted hopefully, looking to- ward the door, as if she thought Bailey might come in any minute.

Gib fought a jab of pain just at the mention of her name.

"Yer never gonna see Bailey again," Kyle said. "Uncle Gib made her go 'way! So there!"

Kate's face pinched up and she turned the grimace to Gib. "Why'd you make her go 'way, Uncle Gib? She was nice to us."

"An' she knowed stuff, too. Good stuff," Kyle added in an accusing tone of his own.

"We've been over this a hundred times since Sunday, and I'm not going over it again! Get into the bathroom so I can wash you both up and clean this room!"

It wasn't the words he spoke but the enraged tone, the decibel level, that stopped everything cold.

Gib had never screamed so fiercely or so harshly at any of the kids—even in the past two days when his patience had been stretched to its limit—and Kate and Kyle froze, their eyes big and wide and frightened. He'd scared Evie, too, because she started to cry as if his anger was directed at her rather than at her brother and sister.

"Man, this is not a happy house," Jack said from the doorway.

Gib hadn't heard his cousin follow him. With Evie crying, Kate's lower lip quivering, Kyle looking as if he wanted to run for the closet he hid in when he thought he was in trouble and the paint mess, Gib didn't know what to address first. He just closed his eyes and shook his head.

"Go on downstairs," Jack said. "Take the beer outside and get some air. I'll clean things up and put the kids back to bed."

This time he accepted his cousin's offer. For the kids' sake, if not for his own.

"Thanks" was all he said to Jack. Then he apologized to Kate and Kyle for losing his temper, kissed Evie on the forehead and left them all behind, mentally beating himself up the whole way down the stairs.

Between the deaths of his brother and sister-in-law and the breakup of his marriage, Gib was no stranger to bad times. But the two days since he'd walked out on Bailey at her office Sunday counted among the worst he'd ever suffered.

He didn't know what he'd expected Bailey to tell him Sunday morning. Maybe that she'd blown up the dryer or didn't know how to toilet train Evie. But the last thing he'd thought she'd been keeping from him was the fact that she was a doctor. That was something he was still having trouble getting used to.

Gib went into the living room, grabbed his beer and took it with him out to the back porch. Sitting on the steps there, he drank nearly half of it, as if that would make him feel better. About the way he'd been with the kids so far this week. About Bailey.

But of course the beer didn't help anything.

He kept replaying Sunday over and over again in his mind, wondering if he'd overreacted.

He'd been thrown for a loop—there was no denying it. First with his parents rushing in with Kate squeaking from the chest and scaring the hell out of him. And then finding out Bailey was an MD on top of it.

That was a big thing to keep a secret. Not that he had some kind of hang-up about women doctors, just that it had been such a shock.

He wondered if it would have been easier to accept the revelations about Bailey if they'd come on their own, at a time when he wasn't dealing with what had seemed like a potential crisis with Kate.

But he didn't think so.

Even without Kate's problem, finding out Bailey was an obstetrician-gynecologist would have floored him.

But he did think that the two shocks coming together had made him a little more upset than he might have been to learn about Bailey's deceptions on their own. A little madder.

And he'd been mad, all right.

Mad that there was so much she'd lied to him about. Mad that she'd lied to him at all. Mad that he hadn't pursued his feeling that she wasn't being straight with him. Mad that he'd had to find out when he was in the middle of an already unnerving situation and with other people there to watch.

But the truth was, what he'd been the most mad about was that everything he learned about Bailey seemed to widen the gap that separated them. Seemed to make it more and more unlikely that they would be able to bridge that gap.

"What a mess," he muttered to himself as he took another long pull on his beer.

Only this mess couldn't just be vacuumed up like sand in the dining room.

He'd let things go too far with Bailey. He knew it and it made him mad all over again. At himself.

What the hell had he been doing Saturday night, taking her to bed when he'd already known there was more to what was going on than she'd led him to believe? When she'd been honest enough to let him know that having a baby of her own was what she wanted more than she wanted anything—something that was a definite no-go with him. When he'd seen her condominium, had a clearer picture of where she was coming from and been wondering how she could leave all of that to be his housekeeper and nanny for any amount of time.

But had he taken any of that into account?

No. He'd let his feelings for her, his desires, have their day because he'd let those go too far, too, and they'd had control of him.

So what if he loved her? So what if he still loved her even now that he knew all the obstacles that stood in their way? So what if every muscle in his body craved the feel of her against him? So what if he could hardly think of anything but her? So what if he'd been on the verge of picking up the phone a hundred times in the past two days to call her and say he didn't give a damn about anything but their being together?

Those feelings, those thoughts, those temptations, didn't change anything, did they? She still wanted her *own* family. She wanted it so much that she'd suspended a whole medical practice and lied to get a job as a nanny and housekeeper just to prepare herself for it.

And he already had his family in place—full, complete, plenty big enough. *Plenty* big enough. He had all he could do meeting the needs of three kids—one of them who now had a health condition he was still worried about.

He and Bailey were just at different places in their lives. They wanted—needed—different things. And he couldn't see anything that could be done about that.

If she took on his kids and gave up having her own, she'd regret it and resent him and the kids—he knew it as certainly as he knew his own name.

And what about taking on more kids himself, when he already felt as if he didn't give Kate, Kyle and Evie enough time, enough attention? He just couldn't do that.

Gib polished off the last of his beer and set the bottle aside as Jack came out of the house and handed him another one.

"Here, I think you need this," his cousin said, sitting beside him on the steps, right where Bailey had sat the night they'd been out here together. The first time Gib had actually kissed her after fantasizing about it for what had seemed like a long time. . . .

He took a hard swallow of his second beer. But it didn't wash away the memory or the pain.

"Are the kids okay?" he asked then.

"Sound asleep. I made sure before I came downstairs. They miss Bailey, though. They think you do, too, and that's why you've been in such a bad mood since Sunday."

"Is that right? Well, I haven't been yelling the way I did tonight, if that's what you're thinking."

"I wasn't. What I was thinking was that you're missing Bailey more the longer you go without seeing her and getting short-tempered because of it."

"Tonight was just a rough night. All the upheaval of Bailey not coming back and the scare over Kate's heart have the kids acting up nonstop. I just lost my patience for it. But I was out of line and it won't happen again. Before I'll scream at them like that, I'll leave the room. I don't care if they're spray painting graffiti on the walls."

"Might just be easier to get Bailey back here and avoid all of you feeling lousy." Gib had told Jack everything that had gone on between him and Bailey.

"Get her back here for a few months until she reopens her practice?" Gib asked skeptically. "What good would that do? Then when she left, we'd all go through this again, only worse because we'd all be more attached to her. Where's the solution in that?"

"I wasn't thinking about rehiring her. I was thinking about getting her back here in a more personal role. Permanently."

Gib stared down at the beer he had dangling by the neck between two fingers. "Wouldn't work," he said, feeling as morose as he sounded. "Wouldn't be fair."

"Why not?"

"Because in order to get her back here permanently, to have a relationship, a life, a future, with her, I'd have to ask her to give up having kids of her own and just raise mine—that sure as hell wouldn't be fair."

"So don't. Have it all—the future, the relationship, the life with her and the kid or two she wants, too."

Gib glanced over at his cousin as if Jack had lost his mind. "I couldn't add more kids to what I have and spread myself even thinner. Kate, Kyle and Evie wouldn't even get the time and attention I'm giving them now and the new ones wouldn't, either. That's not fair to anybody. Plus Bailey is a *doctor,* for crying out loud. How would she be able to keep up with work like that and still deal with three kids, let alone four or five or six? She couldn't do it."

"Did she tell you that?"

"She didn't have to."

"Did you even *ask* her if maybe your three kids might be enough for her?"

Gib shook his head. "She wants her *own*. It's an absolute, nonnegotiable fact of life."

Jack didn't say anything for a while. He drank his beer. They both stared out at the yard.

Then he said, "You know, you're a damn good father, even with your hands full."

"Oh, yeah, I proved that tonight, didn't I?" Gib answered facetiously.

"You lost your temper. Everybody does now and then. Believe me, I've seen worse. Much worse. I've experienced worse. My old man would have hauled off and smacked me black and blue if he'd have come into a mess like you did with Kate and Kyle. You didn't do that. So you raised your voice and it isn't like you. Big deal. Kate, Kyle and Evie are not scarred for life."

Gib didn't respond to that. Nothing his cousin said about it made him feel any better.

Jack went on, anyway. "Those kids are crazy about you. They're happy—well, maybe not right now, but overall, in general. They know they're loved. They get plenty of attention even when things get wild or out of whack or you're in a rush and overwhelmed. I don't know what more you think you could do for them than you're doing."

"Yeah? Well, add a couple more kids to it and see how much attention they get then."

"So you add more kids. You also add a mother for the lot of them."

Gib closed his eyes. "Don't make me feel guilty about Angie's leaving and these kids not having a mother."

"I'm not trying to make you feel guilty. Angie's leaving was Angie's fault, not yours. I'm saying that if you bring Bailey into your life, you won't only be adding the kids she wants, you'll be adding her, too, and giving Kate, Kyle and Evie a mom. Someone else to help take care of them, to fill in the blanks when you can't do everything. Somebody to share the load.

You act as if you'll just be handed a couple more kids to raise on your own—the way these three came to you. But the kids would have Bailey, too. And so would you. Then you could still hire a housekeeper-nanny—what you're going to have to do, at any rate—and it seems to me that things even out. There's enough to go around."

Jack finished that with a flourish, as if he'd just single-handedly solved all Gib's problems.

Gib wasn't so sure about that, even though he wanted to believe it was true. "I don't know," he said dubiously. "You're talking work load. That isn't all that's involved in having kids."

"Don't tell me you're still thinking no woman could love your kids just because Angie couldn't."

Gib thought about that. Bailey had said outright that he was wrong on that count. That she already cared about Kate, Kyle and Evie. And he realized suddenly that he didn't doubt it. He'd seen her affection for them himself. She wasn't anything like Angie had been with them. Angie had been standoffish from the start, and it had never gotten any better. She'd never pulled one of them up into her lap the way Bailey did without even thinking about it. Never connected with them—or let them connect with her—the way Bailey had in just a week's time.

"Or is it you?" Jack asked, interrupting his thoughts. "Don't you think you could love any more kids?"

Gib didn't even need to think about that. "Of course I could love more kids."

"Then maybe it's Bailey you don't love."

He didn't need to think about that, either. But maybe there was something else he should take into consideration.

"It happened so damn fast," he said more to himself than to his cousin.

"Refresh my memory," Jack said sarcastically. "Your folks knew each other for how long before they eloped?"

"Three days."

"And they've been married how many years?"

"Thirty-nine. Forty next month."

"Maybe long-lasting love at first sight is in the genes. Or maybe when it's right, it's right." Jack stood then and slapped Gib on the back. "I'm sleeping on the couch tonight. I've got tomorrow off and I told the kids I'd take them to the zoo to get them out of your hair and you out of theirs. Maybe you ought to spend the time seeing if you can't work things out with a certain doctor over in Cherry Creek."

Gib didn't respond to that one way or another. But what his cousin had said was on his mind as Jack went inside and the silence of the night engulfed Gib.

Everything his cousin had proposed and pointed out sounded good in theory, but theories were easy to come up with. As easy as it was to buzz in here the way Jack did when he had free time, take the kids to the zoo, let them miss their naps, stuff them full of ice cream—and then drop them off at the end of the day for someone else to deal with the stomachaches and overtired tears.

Living with Kate, Kyle and Evie, taking care of them, raising them, nursing the small hurts and the big ones, knowing what was up with them all the time was something else again. Add more kids, and all it meant to Jack was more ice cream to buy.

But it wouldn't be that easy for Gib.

On the other hand, it would be good for Kate, Kyle and Evie to have a mother—he couldn't argue that. There was something about a woman's touch, a woman's attention, that was different from what he could offer them, no matter how hard he tried. He saw it in the way things were between the kids and his mother, the way they'd been with Bailey.

But the idea of parenting more kids still gave him pause.

Sure, having two parents in the house would help. And so would having a good housekeeper and nanny. But what about Kate, Kyle and Evie themselves? Would more kids make them feel displaced? Rejected? Like outsiders, the way he'd thought it would since taking them on as his own? Would he be able to comfort them, to convince them otherwise if the feelings cropped up?

He didn't know. But he did know that if the problem arose he'd bend over backward to reassure them they were as much his kids as any others. Because they were as much his kids as any he might have fathered biologically. He couldn't love them any more than he did. He couldn't enjoy them any more than he did—tonight notwithstanding.

In fact, he loved them and enjoyed them so much that when he thought about it, he realized it might be nice to have just a couple more.

A couple of other little bodies around his when he read the bedtime story. A couple more to tuck in, to kiss good-night. A couple more to run to greet him when he came home from work.

And if that also meant a few more boo-boos to make better? A few more hurts to soothe when he had blueprints to go over or dirty laundry was accumulating all over the place? Maybe a little work piling up wasn't such a high price to pay for so much that was good about having kids. Especially with Bailey by his side.

Because that was where he wanted her. By his side. Through all the work. All the fun. Through everything. And he realized that in every image that had just passed through his mind of having more kids, it was only appealing with Bailey in the picture.

He really did love her. Too much, too deeply for it not to be real just because it had happened so fast.

Too much, too deeply not to have her in his life. In his bed.

Too much, too deeply not to have babies with her.

Way too much, way too deeply to let her have babies with someone else . . .

That thought hit him like a heavyweight fighter's fist.

Bailey with another man? Pregnant by another man? Sharing the experience of giving birth with another man? Raising, enjoying, playing with other kids with another man?

Gib couldn't stand it.

Oh yeah, he loved Bailey. He wanted her. He wanted everything she wanted, no matter what, because he wanted to make her happy. As happy as she made him. She was good for him. They were good together—great together. And she was good for Kate, Kyle and Evie, too, even if she couldn't cook a hot dog or run the washing machine without flooding the floor.

So he was going to do something about it, Gib decided with such conviction that he wondered what had ever held him back.

Not tomorrow while Jack had the kids at the zoo, but now.

Before it was too late.

Because suddenly he knew without a doubt that the only thing that was truly right in the world was for them all to be together.

Bailey had never been good with idle time on her hands. Probably because she'd never had much of it. But with her practice shut down, her former vacation plans canceled, and not working as Gib's housekeeper and nanny, she'd had a lot of idle time since Sunday. A whole lot more than she wanted. More than was good for her, because it left her alone with her thoughts. So many thoughts. And the pain and guilt that came with them.

Lying to Gib had probably been one of the dumbest things she'd ever done. And letting herself fall in love with him had to rank a close second.

But for the life of her, she didn't know how she could have avoided either one.

Sure, she could have told him the truth about herself, about being a doctor, about her lack of experience, about only wanting the job he was offering temporarily to gain some of that experience. But of course he wouldn't have hired her. No one would have. And she never dreamed she'd be so inept.

And as for falling in love with him? She didn't know how she could have stopped it. It had just happened all on its own, against her will, at such a breakneck speed that she hadn't seen it coming.

But despite the fact that she couldn't think of how she might have avoided the lying or the falling in love, it still didn't help how bad she felt. Or the intense sense of loss she was suffering over Gib. Over Kate, Kyle and Evie. It was much, much worse than all the frustration, all her feelings of inadequacy, all the work and weariness of the past week.

She was thinking just that and pacing the floors when her doorbell rang a little after ten that Tuesday night. She hadn't ordered any food delivered and wasn't expecting company, so it alarmed her enough to peek through the peephole in her front door.

The last person she thought to find standing on her stoop was Gib. But that's who it was, handsome enough to make her heart stop, in a black polo shirt and tight jeans, his hair falling on his forehead just the way she liked it best.

She loved the man. She really did. She just didn't know if she should open the door to him.

Why would he be here except maybe to give her a piece of his mind? Or maybe to bring what she'd left behind of her things, and if that was the case she didn't know if she could face the finality of it without embarrassing herself.

He rang the bell again, and she watched him glance in the direction of the living room window, where surely light shone through the pulled drapes. Then he craned his head back to look up at the windows of her second level, where she knew more lights were on, before he tossed a gaze over his shoulder at her car parked at the curb.

He knew she was home. That was the excuse Bailey gave herself for opening the door to him when the truth was that even if what awaited her was an ugly scene or more pain, she couldn't refuse herself the chance to see him again, talk to him, even for only a little while.

"Hi," she said a bit warily when the door was open and she met him eye-to-eye.

"Hi," he greeted her in response.

There was no sign of her suitcase or any of her things, which gave her a moment's relief.

"Can we talk?" Gib asked.

He didn't sound angry, which struck her as another good sign. "Sure. Come on in."

He did that, looking around much the way he had when he'd been here on Saturday night, as if he couldn't believe what he was seeing.

"How are the kids?" Bailey asked both because she wanted to know and to fill the silence he left as he headed for her living room.

"They miss you."

An odd combination of pain and delight went through her at that. "I miss them, too." *And you. Lord, how I miss you....*

Gib didn't sit once he was in the living room. Instead he turned to face her and said, "I can't do much to make them feel any better because I'm suffering from the same thing. In fact, tonight I nearly bit Kate's and Kyle's heads off because I've been in such a lousy mood myself."

"I'm sorry," she said, knowing that if she had never come into their lives they wouldn't be going through this now.

"I didn't come for apologies. Or to make you feel bad. I came to see if we can't work things out."

"Oh," she said, because she didn't know what else to say.

"I meant it when I told you I love you, Bailey. I know it happened fast for us both, but I can't believe it's any less real because of that."

"No, I can't either," she agreed with a small, wry, mirthless laugh.

"Jack gave me a talking-to tonight after I blew up at the kids and made me take a look at the two of us, at what's happened between us. He showed me a new perspective on some things. Like how we could have another baby or two and still be able to meet everybody's needs. Like—"

Bailey listened intently as he outlined a plan for a workable future together, what he was willing to do to accomplish it. And a part of her hung on his every word. But another part of her kept whispering cautions in the back of her mind, reminding her of things she knew she couldn't forget. Her own shortcomings. Failures...

"The bottom line here," he said, "is that I want you to be my wife. To be the mother of the kids I have now and of the kids we have together."

Music to her ears.

And a stab to her heart.

Because Bailey suddenly knew she couldn't have what she wanted most. She couldn't say yes.

"I've had a lot of time to think these past two days, Gib."

"I don't like the sound of that."

"It feels even worse."

"Then don't say it."

"I have to. Last week taught me just how tough a job raising kids is. And just how bad I am at it. I was more of a burden to you than a help—"

"You were anything but a *burden* to me."

"I messed up more than I cleaned and made everything harder and more complicated for you, made more work for you—that's a burden."

"Only if it feels that way, and it didn't. Besides, if you come back, you can still learn and get better at things. And what you and I can't handle together, we'll hire help for."

"But that's not the worst of it," she said slowly, reluctantly, feeling the weight of what she'd had to admit to herself in these two days of thinking. Of what had just now struck her as the truth she couldn't deny. The truth she couldn't let him talk her out of.

"What is the worst of it?"

"As much as I love you—and I *do* love you—I love Kyle and Kate and Evie. But don't you see? They deserve better than I can give them. Better than what I gave them last week. They definitely deserve better as a mom. It wasn't only cleaning and cooking that I cheated them on. It was other things, more important things, *emotional* things."

Gib frowned at her, his expression confused. "What are you talking about?"

"I didn't know what to do when Kyle got upset thinking he might lose you the way he did his parents, when he was scared silly that he'd done something that could drive you away. I didn't know what to do when Kate was feeling sad over her mother. I even scared Kyle more than he already was about Kate's condition on Sunday in Jean's office. I failed them and I'm afraid I'd never have what it takes *not* to fail them when it comes to things like that. I'm afraid I'd fail you." Her voice cracked and she paused to fight against some raw emotions of her own. "I'm even rethinking having any kids at all."

"You are so off base on this," he said, frowning at her, his expression relaying as much disbelief as his tone of voice. "I don't know what you think you did wrong either of those times."

"I didn't help them!" she shouted, her frustration breaking through. "When they really needed me, needed comforting, needed my help, I didn't know what to do. It was much worse than not knowing how to cook or clean. Much more important. And I was at a complete loss."

"Because you didn't totally cure their bad feelings the way you cure infections with antibiotics? I told you when the incident with Kyle and the frog happened that nobody can do that, Bailey. Nobody. There aren't any instant antidotes for the emotions. The best anyone can do is give a little moral support, a lot of love, some compassion and understanding for those bad feelings. And don't tell me you didn't do those things because I know you did."

"It wasn't enough."

"It must have been—they came out of their blue funks, didn't they? And they're crazy about you. Would they be if you'd failed them as much as you think you have?"

She wanted to believe that. Believing it would mean she could accept Gib's proposal.

But she just didn't. Maybe there wasn't a cure for what ailed Kate and Kyle, or any child, for that matter. But surely someone else could have offered more relief than she thought she had. And how, when she was so inept at just being the nanny and housekeeper, could she take on the more important job of mothering Gib's kids? Of being his wife?

She couldn't. She just couldn't. She loved them all too much for that.

"It's no good," she said with a shake of her head. "The kids—*you*—deserve better."

"We all deserve someone who loves us. Or maybe you're a little low on that, too?"

He was angry with her again. But that was better than just being hurt. And if she let him think she didn't love him enough to marry him maybe that was better, too. So she didn't disabuse him of the idea.

"It's just no good, Gib," she said through a throat so tight that the words could hardly pass.

"Tell me it's no good because you don't love me. Because you don't love the kids," he challenged, as if he could read her thoughts.

But faced with needing to say it out loud, to lie to him again, she couldn't do it. All she could manage was "I can't marry you."

It sounded as bad as it felt, as wrenching.

Gib shook his head in disgust. "Not because you don't love me. Not because you don't love the kids. But because you have some inflated idea of what it means to be a wife and mother? Well, you're wrong, Bailey. It's the love that matters. The caring. Nobody is perfect at any of the rest of it."

"Nobody's as bad at it as I am. And we both know it."

"So that's it? You won't marry me?" he demanded with a full head of steam.

"No. I won't."

"Damn it, Bailey—"

"I'm sorry," she repeated, thinking he'd never know *how* sorry.

He stayed standing there, staring at her as if he expected her to change her mind. After a time he said, "Just think about it."

"That's all I have been thinking about."

"So you want me to walk out of here and let that be the end of it."

She couldn't make herself say yes. Instead she only nodded her agreement.

Still he didn't budge. He kept on staring at her, maybe as if he thought that might change her mind. Or maybe because he couldn't believe she meant this.

But when she let silence confirm it, he finally breathed a frustrated, angry breath and headed for the door.

Everything inside of Bailey cried out for him not to go.

But she held it in, for the second time listening to every step that took him away from her.

Only this time he stopped before going all the way out. From the door, to her back, she heard him say, "You're wrong. You're so damn wrong. And we're so damn right together. *All* together."

Bailey didn't turn to face him. She knew she couldn't look at him again and hold her ground. And she needed to. She was sure of it.

He waited, no doubt staring at her back because she thought she could feel the heat of his gaze burning into her. Still she didn't face him, though, willing him to go before her conviction failed her.

And then, finally, she heard him open the door and walk out of her house. Out of her life. And she knew it was over this time. Really, truly over.

Only unlike Sunday in her office, she didn't cry.

She felt too bad even for that.

Chapter Eleven

"I'm sorry I'm late," Jean apologized in greeting as she hurried to the small patio table where Bailey waited for her at the Espresso House. "Kristy called me from school to pick her up. She couldn't finish her last two classes today. I tried to get hold of you to let you know but you'd already left."

Kristy was Jean's fifteen-year-old daughter.

"Is she sick?" Bailey asked, concerned.

"She said she had a stomachache."

"You shouldn't have left her, then. You didn't have to. I was only joking when I said you'd be saving my sanity to give me a reason to get out of the house today. Kristy is more important. Go home."

Jean waved away the suggestion and ordered herself a cappuccino to go with Bailey's latte. Then she said, "Kristy isn't really sick. Her boyfriend broke up with her last weekend and she's heartbroken. She couldn't face her last two classes because he's in them and he won't even look at her. He's busy putting the moves on a new girl. The stomachache was a fake to get herself out of school so she wouldn't have to watch him in action again."

"Shouldn't you be at home with her, anyway?"

"She doesn't need me there while she locks herself in her room, listens to dirges on the CD player and mopes, believe me."

Bailey considered her friend a good, caring, conscientious parent, and it surprised her that Jean was taking this tack in response to her daughter's unhappiness. It also made her curious. Very curious, because in Jean's shoes she'd have felt as if she should be by Kristy's side, working some magic to make Kristy feel better.

Jean's coffee arrived and Bailey waited for her friend to take the first sip before she said, "What are you doing about it?"

"I'm throwing darts at the boy's picture and looking into voodoo curses to cast on him."

"No, I mean about Kristy's broken heart."

"What can I do? I had a talk with her on the way home, but I was probably too soft on her about crying wolf to get out of school. I hurt for her—there's nothing worse than watching your kid in any kind of pain. So I'm pampering her, indulging her more than I should be, giving aid, comfort and support. But that's all I *can* do."

Basically the same things Bailey had done with Kate and Kyle. Which hadn't seemed like enough.

She said as much to Jean, explaining the incidents that had convinced her she was unfit to be a mother. "It wasn't bad enough that I was lousy at all the other motherly kinds of things. When they needed me emotionally, I didn't know what to do, either,'' she finished.

"Oh, Bailey."

"Oh, Jean," Bailey mimicked her friend's near groan.

"Kids have their own stuff to go through. Sometimes you can run interference for them, but most of the time they just have to suffer it—they're *better off* suffering it—just like you and me."

"I don't see how they're better off suffering it. They're only kids."

"Suffering it gets it out of their system. It teaches them a lesson. And even if it's hard to see how Kate's and Kyle's feelings of loss and abandonment are teaching them something, it's still just part of what they need to go through in response to what life's dealt them in order to come out the other end. You can't change that any more than you can change it when one of your patients comes in with a problem pregnancy—you do the best you can to treat it. And it sounds like that's what you did with those kids. No one else could have done anything more for them. I'm Kristy's mother by birth, and I can't take away what she's suffering. That doesn't mean I'm cheating her. Do you think being a mother means you're a miracle worker?"

"I guess maybe I did."

"Well, you were as wrong about that as you were to think having and raising kids would be a snap. You've gone from one extreme to another. And if that's the only reason you turned down Gib Harden's proposal, then you've made a great big mistake, and I'm here to tell you that you're miserable for nothing. Go find him and tell him so."

Bailey wasn't convinced, and she certainly wasn't going to get up from that table and rush to Gib about it—appealing though the idea was. "You just don't know how bad I was at everything," she said, and then changed the subject.

Jean didn't pursue it. She went on to new things, filling Bailey in on the gossip of the past week, discussing some electrical problems they were having at the office, just chatting.

It wasn't until they'd finished their coffee, paid the bill and were headed for the parking lot that Jean said, "You know, Kate's appointment with the pediatric cardiologist over at Children's Hospital is this afternoon. At four."

"How do you know?"

"Roland Taves's nurse called mine this morning to make sure I'd sent the X rays over." Jean checked her watch. "It's three-thirty now. You could probably make it to Children's at about the same time Gib and Kate do."

"They don't need me there."

"Maybe they'd just like to have you there."

Bailey thought about the way she and Gib had parted the night before. "I doubt it."

Jean shrugged as if she'd done all she could and wouldn't push it. But she said, "That three-pound preemie you delivered week before last? Is he still over there?"

"The Russell baby? I'm sure he is. They've had trouble getting him to fatten up."

"You've been following the case?"

"Just calling in."

"So why not pop over there and take a peek at him?"

Which would just happen to put her in the hospital at the same time Gib would be there. Bailey rolled her eyes. "Go home to your heartsick daughter—"

"And quit giving my heartsick friend advice—is that it?"

"I appreciate the advice. But things aren't as simple as you think."

"Or maybe they aren't as complicated as *you* think," Jean said, as she gave Bailey a hug, told her to call if she needed anything and they went their separate ways.

But somehow once Bailey was in her car and on the road again, she just couldn't keep herself from heading in the direction of Children's Hospital rather than the opposite way that would have taken her home.

Jean was right—there was no harm in her checking on the Russell baby.

But even though she tried to pretend that was the real reason she was going, she knew better.

The truth was that now that she was aware of the fact that Kate's appointment with the heart specialist was at hand, she just had to be there. Even if she couldn't actually be with Kate, at least she had to be in the hospital, where she could pay a call on the other doctor afterward, talk to him and make sure Kate's condition wasn't any worse than she thought it was.

And if she ran into Gib along the way?

Well, maybe that wouldn't happen.

The Russell baby had been the last of Bailey's deliveries before closing down her practice. He was only slightly over four pounds now, and after a quick look at his chart and talking to one of the nurse's on duty, Bailey couldn't resist picking him up and rocking him through a fit of crying that turned his cheeks the color of cherries.

It felt good to hold him, to cradle him against her, and as she stared down into the tiny cherub's face she wondered if she really could deny herself having a child of her own.

"Why don't you guys come with instruction manuals?" she whispered to the baby, who had finally grown quiet.

He smiled a smile that looked to Bailey as if it pleased him to know she was confounded, and the thought made her laugh.

After holding the baby a few more minutes, she had a brief consultation with Kate's heart doctor to assure herself there was nothing more seriously wrong with Kate than the mitral valve prolapse. Then Bailey headed for home, thoughtful and melancholy.

Gib was great with those kids. He was a terrific dad to them. He did what Bailey considered all the right things with them. Yet he'd been at as much of a loss as she had.

Was it possible that Gib and Jean had both been right?

Gib had said Bailey had an inflated idea of what it was to be a wife and mother.

Jean had pointed out that mothers weren't miracle workers, that Bailey had gone from one extreme to the other, from thinking that having and raising kids was easy to now believing she had to be able to cure every ill and angst or she wasn't fit to be a parent.

But maybe no one really could cure every ill and angst, maybe she really had developed an inflated idea of what it was to be a wife and mother.

Gib didn't always know what to say to the kids to make things better.

Jean hadn't known how to wipe away the pain of her daughter's broken heart.

So maybe she wasn't so inept after all.

"Or maybe I'm just looking for an excuse so I can have Gib."

Her voice echoed off the art-filled walls, the polished hardwood floor and the emptiness of the place. The longing to be with Gib, in his house, with his family, was so strong inside her that she knew she wanted to believe anything that would get her back there with him. And that made her leery of her own rationalizing.

Yet Jean's remark about Bailey's going from one extreme to another kept replaying itself in her mind.

Wasn't there a happy medium? And wasn't that happy medium being a loving parent who did the best he or she could and still might not always have the answers? A parent who wasn't perfect? Who couldn't work miracles?

It seemed to make sense. It seemed more reasonable than what she'd been expecting of herself.

And if the kids wanted her back? Maybe Gib was right that she must not have failed them too terribly.

So no, she didn't think she was just looking for a way to convince herself it was all right to give in to what she wanted most—to be with Gib.

And that *was* what she wanted most.

Because she loved him. So much she couldn't sleep, couldn't eat, couldn't stop thinking about him, wanting him, wanting to be with him. For the rest of her life.

She loved everything about him. The way he looked. The sound of his voice. The way he held her, kissed her, made love to her. She loved his sense of humor, his patience, his charm. She loved that he was willing to compromise, to do anything he had to for them to be together.

So shouldn't she, too?

And she was. She was willing to do anything at all to have him, she realized suddenly. To have a life, a future, a family, with him.

If he still wanted her. After last night. After today.

But there was only one way to find out.

And that was to go to him and ask.

Bailey didn't go directly to Gib's house. She made one stop first, got waylaid and arrived in the middle of the bedtime mayhem. She could tell even as she climbed the steps to the front porch that that was what was going on inside because the door was open and through the screen came the sounds of the nightly debates over pajamas, and which story Gib was to read, and whether it was to be on Kate's bed or Kyle's, and who had taken out and played last with toys Gib was telling them to put away.

But as she stood there listening, Bailey couldn't help smiling and yearning to be in there, a part of it all.

Sure it was an exasperating routine to go through every evening, and she knew those toys would likely not get put away tonight or even tomorrow and more would be added to them and the mess would pile up and there'd be more and more work trying to get it all under control.

But there wasn't a single thing in the world she'd rather do than be allowed that exasperation, to be a part of all that work. Better that than every bit of the orderliness and quiet in her solitary existence in the cold cavern of that condominium in Cherry Creek.

She raised her finger to the doorbell, but before she had a chance to ring it, Kyle came down the stairs and saw her through the screen. He did a double take, then his eyes grew wide and much like his sister had earlier in the day, he said Bailey's name. Then he turned around and ran as fast as he could back up the stairs, calling his uncle as if the house were on fire.

"Did you let her in?" she heard Gib ask, after Kyle's announcement that Bailey was on the front porch.

"Nooo," the little boy answered, as if she were a ghost and he was too shy to confront her.

Then Kate's voice chimed in, "Where's Bailey? Here? I wanna see her!"

"Don't you go downstairs without your pajamas on!" This from Gib. "Get dressed. I'll be right back."

And down he came with an expression Bailey couldn't read but that certainly didn't seem overjoyed to see her.

"Hi," she said, hating how tentative and unsure of herself she sounded. Then she couldn't think of anything else to say but what he'd said to her the night before. "Can we talk? After the kids are in bed?"

He pushed open the screen door, silently inviting her inside. He had on jeans and that white weight lifter's tank top he'd worn before that left his hard biceps, broad shoulders and part of the front and sides of his chest bare.

She tried not to look because of the fluttery things the sight set off in her stomach. If he'd had enough of her recent hang-ups and had changed his mind about her, she didn't want to have to deal with desire on top of rejection.

She stepped into the entryway as Kate hurried down the stairs, her nightgown on inside out and backward, wearing three necklaces and half a dozen bracelets, too. "You comed back!"

Bailey fought the urge to scoop the child up in her arms, but beyond that she was again at a loss for what to say.

Gib filled in with a stern voice. "Upstairs, Kate. You and Kyle get those building blocks put away and keep an eye on Evie. I need to talk to Bailey alone."

Kate didn't like being dispatched. She scowled at her uncle and put up an argument that she eventually lost. Then to Bailey, as if she were testing her, she said, "Will you be here tomorrow?"

Again Bailey was unsure how to answer that and settled on the truth. "I don't know, honey."

"Go do what I told you, Kate," Gib ordered and after another dirty look tossed his way, his niece stomped off the way she'd come.

Gib held out his arm toward the living room, waiting for Bailey to go ahead of him.

As he followed her, he said, "Does *can we talk* mean you haven't just come to get your things?"

"I guess that's up to you."

He let out a frustrated, confused sort of laugh and shrugged. "What else can I do or agree to that I haven't already?"

From the middle of the living room, she turned to face him. "How about forgiving me?"

"For lying? Done."

"And for being unrealistic about what being a parent involves."

"So you finally see that you *were* unrealistic?"

"Yes. I think so." And she told him why, told him what had opened her eyes.

Then she said, "I was thinking that maybe with more practice, with some counseling, with some parenting classes—" she took out a brochure and schedule that she'd stopped at Children's Hospital to get on her way here and handed them to him "—I could get more confident about what to do with the kids, how to be the best mother I could be and how to recognize a happy medium—"

"*Happy* being the operative word," Gib put in.

"And if I spent the rest of my three months off learning what I set out to learn and then keep my patient load to a minimum, when I go back so my hours aren't too bad, well, maybe we could work things out, after all?"

Through the rush of her own words, she hadn't noticed that Gib was standing there smiling at her. But she noticed it then.

"And do you have a plan for a new baby in all that, too?" he said, his tone edged with the teasing she loved from him.

"I thought we could postpone it for just a little while, until I'm better at everything around here and Evie is out of diapers and—"

"There's more?" He laughed, set down the brochures she'd given him and caught her around the waist to pull her to him.

It was the first time in days that Bailey felt herself relax. She even managed to smile up into his handsome face as she added, "And I come complete with the best housekeeper on earth, who is also wild about kids. Marguerite. She's the bonus. Except that she won't be back to work until I am."

"Well, I was having doubts up to that point, but for a good housekeeper and nanny I'd do about anything."

"Doubts?"

He bent to whisper in her ear, "It was a joke."

"Does that mean we have a deal?"

"Is that what we're making? A deal? I thought we were making a family."

"Right here and now?" she joked back, sounding outrageously suggestive.

Gib glanced sideways to the stairs then back down into her face. "Probably not a good idea since we have an audience."

And they did, too, though Bailey hadn't realized it until just then. But there in the entry were Kate, Kyle and even Evie, standing like three ducks in a row, watching and listening to everything.

"So what do you guys think?" Gib asked as if the kids had the deciding vote. "Should we get married to Bailey and have her be your mom?"

"I a'ready ast'ed her to be *my* mom," Kate announced.

Kyle shrugged one shoulder elaborately. "Sure" was all he said.

And Evie only added, "Bay-we?"

Gib looked into her eyes again. "You *were* talking about marrying me, weren't you?"

"If you'll have me."

"*If* I'll have you?"

"Even though I know more about frogs than vacuum cleaners."

He pretended to think about it. "Yeah, I think I'll have you even then," he said, putting his own suggestive emphasis on *have*.

He looked toward the kids again. "Go on upstairs so I can kiss your mom-to-be and then we'll both come and read your bedtime story."

Kate giggled. Kyle took Evie's hand and the three of them padded off without an argument.

And then Gib did just that—he kissed her. A warm, deep kiss that claimed her as his own, that made her forget there were kids in the house at all, or that there had ever been anything that might have kept her from tasting sweetness like that again.

"I love you," he told her quietly, sincerely, when he'd ended it.

"I love you, too."

"Promise me no more lies. Ever."

"Done."

"And a lifetime together in a house full of kids."

"Well, eventually the kids will grow up, you know, and go out on their own. Then there'll just be you and me."

"Not a bad thought," he said, as if it hadn't occurred to him before. "Then I'll just tell you a few *bedtime* stories."

"My favorite kind. And you're so good at it," she said, matching him innuendo for innuendo.

From upstairs there was more giggling and Kyle hollered down, "You guys done *kissin'* yet?"

"Not yet," Gib called back, even though he was only searching Bailey's eyes with his own. "Shall we do this?"

"Go up to the kids or get married and have a life together?"

"Both."

"Sounds good to me."

Better than he would ever know.

Because Bailey didn't have a doubt that together was what she and Gib were meant to be.

And that all together—she and Gib and Kate and Kyle and Evie and whoever else they might be blessed with along the way—were going to make a great, great family.

* * * * *

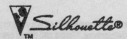

Take 4 bestselling love stories FREE

Plus get a FREE surprise gift!

Special Limited-time Offer

Mail to Silhouette Reader Service™

3010 Walden Avenue
P.O. Box 1867
Buffalo, N.Y. 14240-1867

YES! Please send me 4 free Silhouette Special Edition® novels and my free surprise gift. Then send me 6 brand-new novels every month, which I will receive months before they appear in bookstores. Bill me at the low price of $3.34 each plus 25¢ delivery and applicable sales tax, if any.* That's the complete price and a savings of over 10% off the cover prices—quite a bargain! I understand that accepting the books and gift places me under no obligation ever to buy any books. I can always return a shipment and cancel at any time. Even if I never buy another book from Silhouette, the 4 free books and the surprise gift are mine to keep forever.

235 BPA A3UV

Name	(PLEASE PRINT)

Address	Apt. No.

City	State	Zip

This offer is limited to one order per household and not valid to present Silhouette Special Edition® subscribers. *Terms and prices are subject to change without notice. Sales tax applicable in N.Y.

FORTUNE'S Children™

Bestselling Author
BARBARA BOSWELL

Continues the twelve-book series—FORTUNE'S CHILDREN—
in October 1996 with Book Four

STAND-IN BRIDE

When Fortune Company executive Michael Fortune needed help
warding off female admirers after being named one of the ten most
eligible bachelors in the United States, he turned to his faithful
assistant, Julia Chandler. Julia agreed to a pretend engagement, but
what starts as a charade produces an unexpected Fortune heir....

MEET THE FORTUNES—a family whose legacy is greater than riches.
Because where there's a will...there's a *wedding!*

"Ms. Boswell is one of those rare treasures who combines humor
and romance into sheer magic."
—*Rave Reviews*

A CASTING CALL TO
ALL FORTUNE'S CHILDREN FANS!
If you are truly one of the fortunate
you may win a trip to
Los Angeles to audition for
Wheel of Fortune®. Look for
details in all retail Fortune's Children titles!

Look us up on-line at: http://www.romance.net   FC-4-C

As seen on TV!
Free Gift Offer

With a Free Gift proof-of-purchase from any Silhouette® book,
you can receive a beautiful cubic zirconia pendant.

This gorgeous marquise-shaped stone is a genuine cubic
zirconia—accented by an 18" gold tone necklace.

(Approximate retail value $19.95)

Send for yours today...
compliments of ▼ *Silhouette*®

To receive your free gift, a cubic zirconia pendant, send us one original proof-of-
purchase, photocopies not accepted, from the back of any Silhouette Romance™,
Silhouette Desire®, Silhouette Special Edition®, Silhouette Intimate Moments®
or Silhouette Yours Truly™ title available in August, September or October at your favorite
retail outlet, together with the Free Gift Certificate, plus a check or money order for
$1.65 U.S./$2.15 CAN. (do not send cash) to cover postage and handling, payable
to Silhouette Free Gift Offer. We will send you the specified gift. Allow 6 to 8 weeks for
delivery. Offer good until October 31, 1996 or while quantities last. Offer valid in the
U.S. and Canada only.

Free Gift Certificate

Name: _____

Address: _____

City: _____ State/Province: _____ Zip/Postal Code: _____

Mail this certificate, one proof-of-purchase and a check or money order for postage
and handling to: SILHOUETTE FREE GIFT OFFER 1996. In the U.S.: 3010 Walden
Avenue, P.O. Box 9077, Buffalo NY 14269-9077. In Canada: P.O. Box 613, Fort Erie,
Ontario L2Z 5X3.

FREE GIFT OFFER
084-KMD
ONE PROOF-OF-PURCHASE
To collect your fabulous FREE GIFT, a cubic zirconia pendant, you must include this
original proof-of-purchase for each gift with the properly completed Free Gift Certificate.

084-KMD

The collection of the year!
NEW YORK TIMES BESTSELLING AUTHORS

Linda Lael Miller
Wild About Harry

Janet Dailey
Sweet Promise

Elizabeth Lowell
Reckless Love

Penny Jordan
Love's Choices

and featuring
Nora Roberts
The Calhoun Women

NEW YORK

MARQUIS

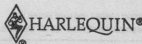 

NYT1296-R

You're About to Become a *Privileged Woman*

Reap the rewards of fabulous free gifts and benefits with proofs-of-purchase from Silhouette and Harlequin books

Pages & Privileges™

It's our way of thanking you for buying our books at your favorite retail stores.

PROOF OF PURCHASE
Offer expires October 31, 1996
SSE-PP183

Pages & Privileges™

**Harlequin and Silhouette—
the most privileged readers in the world!**

For more information about Harlequin and Silhouette's PAGES & PRIVILEGES program call the Pages & Privileges Benefits Desk: 1-503-794-2499

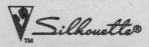

Silhouette®

SSE-PP183